MW00679218

SLOW BURN

IRON HORSE SERIES

DANIELLE NORMAN

Copyright © 2018 by Danielle Norman
and F Squared, LLP
All rights reserved.

Without limiting the rights under the copyright reserved above, no part of
this publication may be reproduced, stored in or introduced into a retrieval
system, or transmitted, in any form, or by any means (electronic, mechanical,
photocopying, recording, or otherwise) without the prior written permission
from either the author and or the above named publisher of this book with
the exception for the use of brief quotations in a book review.

This is a work of fiction. Names and characters are the product of the
author's imagination. The author acknowledges the trademarked status and
trademark owners of various products referenced in this work of fiction.

If you feel that you resemble any part of this story, it is purely coincidental.
And depending on which part, the author recommends either standing in line
with the other one-billion people that also have the same day to day life
experiences, or seeking mental help.

I'd like to dedicate this to all the bad moms especially the one on the airline who allowed their child to take a shit on the plane...ARE YOU FUCKING KIDDING ME?

1) Your child is now forever known as the public shitting kid because of you. Those photos and that story will live on forever. That embarrassment will come back to haunt them and they will only have you to blame. For once think about future repercussions on your child's psyche.

2) No one and I mean no one should have to see or smell your child's SHIT. Get your lazy ass up and take them to the restroom just like everyone else. Have some respect.

And finally...

3) Ummmm, I'll take hygiene for $5,000 Alex.

Your soulmate is the person that mends your broken heart by giving you theirs.

~Unknown

PROLOGUE

*T*wenty years ago . . .

Grabbing Rainbow Dash, my favorite My Little Pony, I tiptoed to my bedroom door to see what was going on. Mommy and Daddy were talking.

"Cora, don't do this. You can't. What about the girls?"

"I have to, Samuel. Every day that I stay here, I die a little more inside. I wasn't meant to be a farming wife. I was made for more."

"You can't keep doing this. You run off for a week, and when you run out of money, you come crawling back, begging for forgiveness. I don't know what happened to you, but you aren't the same woman I married, the woman who used to be my best friend. That woman wouldn't walk out on me or her kids."

"That's the problem, Samuel, we've only ever been friends. I want more. I want passion. I want to be swept off my feet. Friends don't do that."

Standing quietly in the shadow of the hallway, I prayed that no one would see me, because, if no one saw me, then this might all be a nightmare. I squeezed my eyes tightly

1

closed and listened as Mommy and Daddy continued to argue. As Daddy asked Mommy to stay for London, for me, for my baby sister Holland. Mommy didn't care. Nothing would make Mommy stay when she wanted to go.

"Cora, I love you. I always have, but if you leave, you'll never be able to put us back together again."

Don't leave, Mommy, don't leave. Don't leave, Mommy, don't leave.

Over and over, I chanted, not opening my eyes. I was afraid that if I did, she'd be gone, and all my praying would have been for nothing.

Everything went silent. I could hear the bullfrogs croaking outside and an owl hooting, but Mommy and Daddy weren't arguing anymore. Bringing Rainbow Dash up to my face, I peered through her pastel-colored mane that tickled my nose and found Mommy standing right in front of me. I loved Mommy, and if she left, who'd read me my bedtime stories or make dinner?

Mommy closed her eyes and dropped her handbag and box before bending so we were eye to eye. She wiped away the tears that were still rolling down my cheeks.

"I'm sorry, Paris. I am so, so sorry." For the first time that evening, Mommy wasn't screaming. Maybe she was going to cry too, but she didn't. She placed her hand around the back of my neck and brought my head to hers so our foreheads were pressed together. "Mommy has to go. I know you don't understand this, but I can't be happy here. You want Mommy to be happy, don't you?"

I nodded, but I wasn't sure if I wanted to say yes. Not if it meant Mommy would leave.

"But just because Mommy isn't here, it doesn't mean that I don't love you—"

"And London and Holland too?"

"Yes, that means London and Holland too. You take care

of Daddy, okay? I need you to step up and do some of the stuff that I did. Can you do that for me?"

Even though I was only seven, Mommy's words made me feel bigger. She thought I was big enough to do some of her stuff? "Do you mean like making cookies, Mommy? I can't do big cooking yet, but I promise I will when I'm grown. Will that make you happy, Mommy?" Hiccupping between my tears, I locked eyes with her, hoping that she'd tell me what I had to do. Mommy had shown me how to pick the weeds out of the garden, so I could already do that. I knew Daddy liked hugs, so I'd hug him lots and lots. I knew that London and Holland liked cookies, so I could do that too.

"Yes, Paris, that will make Mommy very happy." Mommy smiled, and I liked it when Mommy smiled. Maybe she'd come back tomorrow and smile like that again.

"Okay, Mommy. I can do your stuffs and take care of Daddy and London and Holland."

PARIS

*I*t was bad enough having to tell one of your sisters they had a wedgie—or worse, camel toe—but to actually see said camel toe . . . ummm . . . nah. Giving myself a mental shake, I cleared my mind and mumbled all the crap that people liked to spew. *This is natural.*

In my twenty-eight years, I'd seen lots of horses and cows being examined when they were giving birth. I should be able to handle my sister, right? Wrong. So, so wrong.

"Don't push yet," Meghan, the midwife London hired, instructed. "Paris, why don't you massage London's stomach? Right along the waistband area." I moved to the side and gently kneaded my fingers across her stomach, occasionally catching glimpses of the carnage—or what would soon be carnage, after a baby came out.

"Is this almost over yet?" London whimpered.

"Tell me again why you wanted to have a baby at home?" I looked at her, totally perplexed.

"Actually, you, it's all your fault. You were the one who convinced me to do this."

"Me? How did I do that? I never said have a baby at home."

"No, it was all your talk about being a mom, providing the best for your children. That's what I'm doing, this is supposed to be the best."

"Are you nuts? Pain isn't what's best. Forcing your sister to act as your doula isn't what's best, it's just cruel and unusual punishment."

London moaned in pain and panted through another contraction before her eyes cut back to me. "Are you fucking kidding me? Hell no, if I'm going to be miserable, then all of you can be miserable with me. Where's Holland? She should be miserable too."

Our youngest sister had found a way to escape the monstrosity that was the birthing room. "Umm, I think she's trying to do everyone's chores around the ranch, since you have us all in here."

"Oh. Okay, then."

London's husband, Braden, along with Holland and myself had spent the last month trying to turn what had once been London's old room into a nursery suite.

With Braden's work schedule as a deputy, the chores on the ranch that still had to get done whether there was a baby or not, and the stress once the baby arrived, London and Braden had decided it would be easier if they stayed at the big house, that was what we all called this home. We all referred to theirs as the little house, which was weird, since their house was still almost three thousand square feet.

Originally, I'd been excited by the thought of having my sister back here again, but a twinge in my chest had me questioning my thoughts. Holland ran the stables, and Wally and Jack took care of the cattle. That left me to help take care of the baby when needed.

For the first time ever, I was regretting that. God, I was such an awful person for feeling this way.

"You're at nine centimeters, London, it won't be much longer now." Meghan moved to wash her hands in the ensuite bathroom.

"Nine? Did you say nine? Are you sure it isn't nine hundred? I've been here forever."

Braden rubbed an ice chip across her temple and behind her ears, which had her closing her eyes in bliss. "God, that feels so fucking good."

"You probably shouldn't use the lord's name and the word *fuck* in the same sentence." I giggled.

"Christ on a cracker. Will you shut the holy fuck up? Don't tell me what I can or cannot say. I'd like to see you in my position. You know what? That's a great idea. You get over here and do this, I'm done." London moved to sit up.

"Umm, honey. Stay in bed."

"I can't, Braden, I'm tired. I don't want to do this anymore."

He shot me a pleading glance, but he was on his own for this one. If she thought she could quit in the ninth hour, more power to her.

"You don't have a choice, it's almost over."

"Listen to me right now, Paris, I don't care what anyone tells you, all the bullshit about it not hurting, they'll just stick it in for a second. Yeah, right! And nine months later, you are screaming your head off and shooting a watermelon out your hooha. It is so not worth it—" Whatever else London was going to say was cut off by another contraction. "Ouuuwww."

Braden fought the urge to laugh, but failed, and when London looked as if she might lunge at him, Meghan stepped in.

"London, you have this." Meghan's voice was as calm as the ocean when there were red skies at night.

For hours, this had been the pattern: London would get pissed off, I would try to calm her and help soothe her aching muscles, Braden would say something stupid, and she would yell. I did everything I could think of to make her more comfortable; after all, it was London who'd been in labor for almost eighteen hours.

"What time is it?" London sounded exhausted when she asked that for what had to be the tenth time.

"It's almost two. Just relax, darling. Our baby will be here soon." Braden wiped the hair away from London's brow.

"Relax? You want me to fucking relax when I'm shoving a kid out of my vagina? An area that, I might add, you find, or did find, tight—"

"Okay, London." I held up my hands and nearly shouted. Witnessing my sister giving birth was one thing, but hearing about her sex life, that was a hard no.

"Mom, are you ready? I think this little one is tired and wants to get out." Meghan's voice silenced us. London, who'd seconds ago been ready to snap Braden's head off, turned into a sweet, caring woman, ready to hold her baby. "You're fully effaced." Meghan grinned up at London, then over to Braden. "Dad, let's keep Mom calm and just focus on bringing this beautiful baby into the world." Meghan moved the sheet that was splayed across London's knees. "London, I want you to relax, tell me, what names have you picked out?" Oh, she was good. The woman could deliver a baby, keep a mom from killing the dad, and try to soothe a frantic new mother all at the same time.

"Samuel if it's a boy, after my dad . . ."

"Okay, push for me, London."

Braden wrapped one arm around London's shoulders and hooked his other under one of her knees while I backed away. I couldn't do this, I couldn't explain it, but I just couldn't be here. I didn't want to see this. Oh my god. The first tear fell down my face, then the second, and the third. I was seconds away from everyone noticing, from pulling attention away from the one person who truly deserved it today.

"I don't feel so well. I'll be back." I rushed from the room and through the house.

Our home was like a giant wagon wheel. The center was where the living room, dining room, and kitchen all joined together in an open floor plan. But from there, hallways that resembled spokes radiated out, giving each of us our own wing, so to speak.

When I hit the living room and Holland was nowhere to be seen, I kept running, out the door, down the front steps, and all the way to the stables. When I was young, I used to run away from home often, well . . . run away all the way to the barn, where my horse was tethered. Feeling like a scared little girl who'd had her feelings hurt, I raced into Ursula's stall, buried my face into her blonde mane, and inhaled. What was happening to me? I was the one who had wanted to be a mom ever since she was seven, and I couldn't even watch my sister give birth? I mentally bashed myself for my actions.

Ursula's gentle snort was all the comfort I needed at that moment. At one time, it would have been my dad's hand rubbing my back, assuring me that everything would be all right. I could hear him now.

"You take everything so personal, Paris Jean, you're so much like your mother. London didn't mean to hurt your feelings."

Or he'd pull me against him, giving off that smell of smoke I used to hate, but would have done anything to smell again, and tell me, *"You watch your television shows and think all families are perfect, but they aren't. The only thing that is perfect is that this family is perfect for you, no one else, just you."*

Was I really so much like my mother? What was happening to me? Who was I? I inhaled the earthy scent of hay.

No. I needed to get my shit together, but I wasn't thinking right. I was jealous, that was all. Just normal jealousy. Straightening myself, I wiped my face and tried to analyze what I was feeling, but it didn't work, no matter what I tried. The truth was, I wanted to shout at my sister, scream, ask her why, why her? Why did she get the happily ever after? Why did she get the husband, the baby, the house that was all hers to decorate?

This life was not for me, I wasn't meant to be around people who were happy, because it seemed as if I was destined to be alone for the rest of my life. I was going to grow into a bitter woman . . . just like my mom.

"Paris!"

I flung myself through the stall door then out the stables and back up to the house. Taking the porch steps two at a time, I swung open the front door and hightailed it down the corridor to London's room.

The moment I stepped into the room, a part of my heart cracked, solidifying my feelings. Yup, I was a horrid person. I was full of jealousy. This had been my dream. The husband, the baby, the family. It took my breath away. I was happy for her, truly I was, but I was also envious.

"Come see your niece." I walked toward my sister and her daughter. "Paris, I'd like you to meet Tera Kelly McManus. Tera, this is your aunty Paris."

"Hello, little one. You have no clue, but you are going to be one spoiled little girl." Tera was truly adorable, with her tiny tuft of dark hair. She had Braden's hair, not our reddish blonde. At least she would match her dad. It could be worse

—like Asher, who seemed to have the same hair color as his Golden Retriever.

"How much does she weigh?"

Meghan answered, reading the statistics off a chart. "Miss Tera arrived at four thirty-two, she was twenty inches long, and weighed seven pounds ten ounces. Her skin is rosy, and from everything that I can see, she is absolutely perfect."

"Yes, she is," I murmured as I stared down at the baby before smiling and looking to my sister as she gazed down at her newborn. "Happy Mother's Day."

"Oh my god, I totally forgot, little one. Today is my first Mother's Day, and that's all because of you. You are the best Mother's Day present ever," London cooed to Tera. "Oh, my little Tera, I'm going to be the very best mom in the world. You'll never wonder where I am, or if I'm coming home to you." London's words pierced me, because she was describing our own mother. And having watched London these past nine months, I knew without a shadow of a doubt that she was right, she'd be nothing like Cora Kelly.

But me? I wasn't so sure. I was so determined not to be like her that maybe I overlooked the fact that I truly was more like her than I'd realized. Cora had always been so jealous of what everyone else had. My memories of her were few, but the ones I had seemed like they were just yesterday.

Emotions ripped through me as I remembered one scene perfectly. "Hi, Mommy." I waved as I jumped out of my friend Cara's car when they'd dropped me off after a sleepover. "Isn't their car nice? Cara's daddy surprised her mommy with it. It was an versary present."

"Anniversary."

"Yeah, that's what I said. He put a big bow on it. And when Cara's mommy was gone to get her and her brothers from school, he brought it to their house. When they arrived home, she saw it. Cara's mommy cried."

"Did they do all of that in front of you?" I remember my mom looking so pissed, and I was scared that I'd said something wrong.

"No. Cara just told me about it. It happened a few days before me."

"They've always been such show-offs. Good god, she probably told Cara to tell you the story just so I'd hear about it. She's always bragging."

I was never allowed to go over to Cara's after that, and eventually Cara stopped being my friend. I shook my head to try to shake away the sad memory. Was I like that? Was I jealous of what other people had? Yes, I was. I was jealous of my own sister. I mean, what kind of person couldn't even be happy for her own sister? Would I start to resent her and the baby? Oh my god, what if I resented my own kids?

Our mom had named us after places she loved, places she dreamed about, but somewhere along the way we had become a constant reminder of what she didn't have: a life of adventure and travels.

"Penny for your thoughts."

I blinked and looked away from the baby, who had been smacking her tiny pink lips in her sleep, only to find that both London and Holland were looking at me with curiosity.

Had I missed something?

Braden cleared his throat and held the camera up a bit.

Oh, right.

"Crap. You all are waiting on me, sorry." I curled up next to London, one arm draped over the top of her head and the other placed carefully on Tera, and I smiled as Braden snapped the photo of the next generation of Kelly women. When I stood, London held on to my arm.

"What's on your mind?"

I couldn't discuss this with her. I couldn't tell her that I was jealous of her and worried that I might be more like

Cora than any of us would like to admit. So, I went with the obvious. "I'm just thinking about how much I miss Dad. I wish he could have been here. He'd have been the world's greatest Gramps."

"Holy cow, our little Tera would want for nothing if Daddy were still around." Holland held on to the baby's hand.

"I think Braden's dad is going to help fill that void." London smiled up at her husband.

"Oh crap." I jumped up and moved toward Braden. "Give me that camera, let me get some pictures of the three of you." I waited for Braden as he placed his palm over London's, and together they held Tera's tiny fist in their joined hands, a sign of unity and protection, and then I snapped the photo.

Braden moved to lay alongside London, one strong arm across her as he looked down at his wife and daughter.

"Look at the little family," Holland said as Braden bent to kiss London's forehead. "Y'all are so perfect." *Did she know she was crushing my heart?* "Tera, you have the world's greatest mom." Each comment sliced through what felt like already open flesh, but I hid it all behind the snapping of the camera's shutter.

A few dozen pictures later, I handed the camera to Holland and mustered up a small smile. "I'm going to text Asher and Marcus, I'm sure they're dying for news. Then I'll have some food ready soon." I strolled out of the room and pulled out my phone. Finding Asher's name, I sent a message to him and his brother, Marcus.

ME: Mom and baby are fine. Tera Kelly was born at 4:32

I slid the phone back into my pocket and headed to the kitchen, wanting nothing more than to get lost in the act of cooking.

* * *

THE KITCHEN HAD ALWAYS BEEN my safe haven, and the cool yellow tones on the walls with tiny strawberries painted along the top gave it a homey feel. Well, it always made me feel at home, my sisters not so much. They'd rather be anywhere but in the kitchen unless, of course, I was calling them to eat.

"Shit." The oatmeal chocolate chip cookie flew across the kitchen as I flung the spatula in the air, scared to death. I turned to see who or what had just poked me, but no one was there, so I spun the other way.

Asher.

The man had a cookie in his mouth and three in his hand already.

"Busted. Put those down, mister. No cookies for you." I waved the spatula and barked the command, similar to the Soup Nazi from *Seinfeld*. "How in the hell am I going to make enough if people keep snagging them?"

"It's totally your fault. You told me I was welcome to help myself. Besides, you make the best damn cookies." Asher finished the first cookie completely unrepentantly. "You and I both know that, if I search this kitchen, I would find another jar of cookies hidden. You keep this one out because you want everyone to come by. But you would never want to run out, since your sisters love them, and you are a people pleaser. I know you too well, Paris Jean Kelly. Admit it, you have another jar hidden, don't you?"

I locked eyes with Asher; his blue eyes were so light, I used to think I could look straight into his head and see exactly what he was thinking. That was, of course, until I learned I was wrong, it wasn't his eyes that gave him away— it was his mouth. He couldn't control his smile. The slight quiver meant he was making fun of me.

"No, I do not." I was happy to prove him wrong.

"You don't?" Asher's smile fell.

"Nope. See, you don't know everything, Asher Kinkaide." I turned my head and placed a hand over my mouth to cover my smile. "I have two hidden."

"Ahh, you brat."

I giggled. Asher always could make me smile, even when I was seriously beating myself up.

He reached behind me and grabbed another cookie. "How's Braden holding up?"

"As well as we could hope after having to watch London in labor for so long. Every time one of his girls makes a noise, he freaks. He doesn't want London to strain herself, he's flipping through every how-to book for new fathers, and he's checking Tera every five minutes just to make sure she's breathing."

"Besides how-to books, is there anything else they need?"

"No, Braden has been planning for this day forever. He has put every childproof cover on everything and locks on every damn cabinet. I swear to god, I'm going to murder him. I can't even figure out some of these damn contraptions."

"What about London?"

"Oh, don't worry about her. Braden is waiting on her hand and foot. I'm surprised he isn't following her to the bathroom to wipe her ass."

"Gross." Asher shook his head. "How about the baby? Do they need anything for her? My mom made her several blankets; you know how she still loves to knit. I'll bring them over later."

I stared at him, dumbfounded. "Tell her thank you. But remember, this is Braden, the man with his own library of parenting magazines, you realize that, right? He had wanted London for a long time, and now that he's finally got his dream woman, believe me, having a baby with her only made him that much more whipped. There is nothing they need. He's been buying constantly, I think as a way to prove he is worthy or something, I don't know. Anyway, for the last nine months boxes have been arriving from Children's Place, Amazon, Babies R Us, you name it. I asked him if he was saving all of the packing peanuts as well."

"Why?"

"So he could wrap the baby in them. He was acting so protective over London while she was pregnant that I could only imagine how he'd be with Tera."

"He isn't going to allow her to date until she's forty, is he?"

I smiled at that thought. My dad used to say we couldn't date until we were forty either. "Really? You think he'll let her date then?"

Asher bumped my shoulder. "How about you? How you holding up?"

"Right as rain. You know me."

"Yep, and that's why I'm asking. You are my soft soul." Asher wrapped one arm around me and squeezed.

God, I loved when he did it, because I felt so safe and protected. Asher and I had been friends since . . . well, since we came home from the hospital. Our friendship was the most valuable thing I owned. I'd do anything to protect it. Often times, I wondered if I'd ever find this same feeling with a guy who I burned passionately for, someone other than my best friend, someone who loved me and wanted to have a family with me.

I may be starting to think I was like her, but at least I could learn from her mistake and not mix love and friendship. Though, if I were ever going to do it, I would cross that line with Asher.

"I wish Daddy were here. He probably wouldn't be

shocked to know it was a girl, since it seems the Kelly ranch is destined to be all girls."

"I miss him too, but he's here, he sees her, I'm sure." Asher pulled me in a little tighter. "You know, he was always good to Marcus and me. And after my dad died, he'd call and check in on us to see if we had 'guy stuff' to discuss."

I fought back my laugh. I loved how Asher could bring me out of my pity party. "Yeah, London and I overheard him and Wally talking one day. London threatened to tell Daddy I had tried cigarettes if I ever told you I overheard what they talked to you about. Even though he smoked like a chimney, I knew he'd bust my ass, since we were not allowed to hang around the corral area. I guess that's where all of them went to talk about things not appropriate for little ears." The memory warmed me inside.

"What did you overhear?" Asher leaned back, mirth crinkling in the corners of his eyes.

"He and Wally were talking about how old you and Marcus were. It was right when Marcus started driving. He figured that someone needed to talk to you boys about sex. London had to explain to me what that was."

Asher cracked up laughing. "I remember that conversation. I'm not sure if your dad was more uncomfortable or if I was. But he took Marcus and I out fishing and handed us each a beer." Asher's eyes were brighter than I'd seen in a long time as he remembered the event.

"Seriously?"

"Yeah, but they were those non-alcoholic ones, and they tasted like piss water. Anyway, he stuttered so many times before Marcus finally came clean and explained that he'd already had the talk with me. I think your dad was relieved."

I smiled. Asher is probably talking about the same look my dad had on his face when he explained periods to London and me. He never liked discussing personal stuff, so when it came time to tell Holland, London and I took pity on him and did it for him.

Asher and I were silent for a few minutes before he placed a quick kiss on the top of my head. "What else is on your mind?" His words were warm against my scalp.

"Nothing."

"Something is, I can see it written all across your face. Don't worry about me, you know you can talk to me about anything. I'm always here for you."

"I know. You're my best friend, and I appreciate you." I let out a forced laugh. "Just do me a favor, okay?"

"Anything."

"Whenever you find the one, please make sure she lets us still be friends."

"Yeah, okay." Asher's words were curt as he pulled his arm back. It wasn't exactly the response I expected, but I let it slide as I watched him retreat out the back door.

I was still staring after him, wondering what I'd said, when the buzzer on the oven went off, and then I was back to work, pulling out more fresh cookies.

ASHER

*P*aris lifted the curry brush high above her head, and my mind was instantly in the gutter. Like I'd fantasized a million times since I was a teenager and had seen my first B-rated porno, I expected her to thrash her hair around, and then the brush to miraculously turn into a sponge. At which point, she'd then rub it over the front of her body and allow the water to trickle down the front of her shirt, giving me a good view of her breasts. Because let's face it, if I was dreaming, I was going the whole way, the hot car wash, sunshine cascading down.

"Asher, you're here."

Fuck. Trying to get my mind anywhere other than where it had just been, I paused to give my erection a few seconds to go down. "Yep. Sorry it's so early."

"I'm just grateful you came. I don't know what I'd do without you."

I opened the door to the stall and moved next to Ursula. The smooth palomino coat of the mare felt like velvet as I ran my fingers along her back hock. I had a special bond with Ursula, after all, she was Paris's horse, and as soon as she'd told me that Ursula was limping, she became a priority.

"What do you think?" Paris held her arms tight around her body, rocking with worry.

"It's swollen but doesn't feel as if she's dislocated anything. I'm going to take an X-ray just to be sure." I stopped next to Paris and stared into her gorgeous eyes. I'd been hypnotized by them for most of my life. Tucking a strand of hair behind her ear, I leaned forward and kissed her forehead. "Don't worry. You know that I'll do whatever I can for Ursula."

"That's because you're a good doctor."

"That's because she's your horse and you love her." I headed off to my truck without saying another word and grabbed my portable X-ray unit. The thing was old, and I knew there were more compact versions that weren't so cumbersome, but this one was paid for. And as a new veterinarian who had his eye on starting a family, I was watching my finances.

When I returned to the stables, Paris was cooing to her horse, and Ursula was leaning into her, soaking up the peace and love that Paris offered. I was frozen, mesmerized by this woman who I was in love with; she was everything I'd ever wanted. I just needed to take that step forward and tell her.

Paris held Ursula while I quickly positioned the machine and snapped the photo. We waited while the film developed and were pleased with the results. As I had expected, it was a sprain. After carefully wrapping the joint, I reloaded my truck and then sat on the tailgate.

"How's everything in the house going? Tera keeping you awake?"

"No, she's a really good baby." Paris came over and hopped up next to me.

It was just after seven in the morning, and already the air

felt like a sauna. It was heavy and humid. Paris reached up to wipe her brow and then leaned over and rested her head on my shoulder.

"I'm going to hate when they move back to their house. Everything seems so alive right now, someone is always coming or going. When it's just Holland and me, the place felt like a mortuary. Everything reminds me of my dad. Besides, Holland is never here, she sleeps and eats in the house, but that's about it."

"You could always start your own family." The words slid out of my mouth, and before I could take them back, the rightness of them seemed to take hold, so I left them there, just floating in the air. But Paris didn't even acknowledge me.

She swung her legs, her head resting on my shoulder. Reaching up, I cupped her face in my hand and held her there in the crook of my shoulder. Everything felt so right about this moment.

"After Dad died, people kept saying, 'Give it time. Time heals all wounds,' but you know what?"

"What?" My voice was more of a whisper.

"They were wrong. Time doesn't heal. It only changes how you feel. I still miss him every day, but instead of hurting because he's gone, I'm filled with memories of happy times. Does that make sense?"

"Yeah, total sense." She had no clue how apropos her statement truly was, time changed how we felt. For me, it intensified my love for her.

Paris swayed to the rhythm of her legs swinging back and forth. "Do you remember when we'd stay up late and watch old Elvis Presley movies with your mom?"

"Yeah." I chuckled, just thinking about the memories and how I thought Elvis was so stupid, wasting time with girls instead of surfing in Hawaii.

My heart skipped when she sang the first few notes of a

21

song that she used to sing when we were kids. It had been from one of the movies.

"Which movie was that from?"

Paris sat up and feigned offense. "How dare you forget. It's from *Bye Bye Birdie*, the movie based on Elvis getting drafted into the Army... I love you, Asher, oh yes I dooooo." Her words were soft, but each one warmed me and reminded me that this was us, this comfort. We'd been like this since we were toddlers...comfortable with each other. "I love you, Asher, and I'll be true. When I'm not with you, I'm blue. Oh Asher, I love you." She finished the original part of the ditty, and just like always, being a boy and not wanting to end on mushiness, I added my line.

"Cha cha cha." It was the same line my dad used to say.

"Don't ever leave me, Asher. I don't know what I'd do without you."

"Not going anywhere, kitten."

"Promise?"

"Promise. Well . . ."

"See? You're already being fickle." Paris had a hint of mischief in her voice.

"I have to get to work. I swung by here before the start of my day, but I need to make money if you expect me to stay around and take care of you."

"Oh, well, when you say it that way, I guess you can leave for a little while."

I jumped down, then helped Paris off the tailgate before closing up. Leaning forward, I placed a kiss on the top of her head and watched as she headed toward the house. Then, getting into my truck, I headed to my official first appointment of the day.

By late afternoon, I was at the home of my second dog of the day, Captain, a thirteen-year-old Great Pyrenees that weighed almost one hundred forty pounds. I knelt in the barn and examined him. He was clearly in pain because of the moderate hip dysplasia, which wasn't all that uncommon in dogs his size. Truth be told, thirteen years old was ancient for his breed.

But he was all the owner had, so I did what I could and gave him a shot of an anti-inflammatory into his hips and piggybacked it with painkillers.

"Thank you so much for coming out, Asher." Mr. Howard extended a hand, which I shook.

"Here's some Rimadyl. Remember, it's easier to maintain the pain than to play catch-up. So, set a timer on your phone if you have to, but try to give this to him every six hours. If he's still having problems, you know you can call me anytime, no matter the hour."

I leaned down and rubbed Captain on the head, something all dogs seemed to love, and his back leg twitched. Good. He still had muscle-nerve reflex.

"I know I can. You're just a great doc, just like your father was."

I was appreciative that so many of Dad's clients had returned to me once I had graduated from the University of Florida. Sure, it was nice having a ready-made business and a last name people trusted. But for folks in this part, I was a convenience. No one wanted to haul an old dirty dog in the back of their car. And farm animals were out of the question, especially when we were thirty minutes from the next town. Most large-animal vets only came to this area once a month, which was one day too many for my dad.

"Thanks. I do try. You have a good night, Mr. Howard. And remember to call if you need to." With that, I picked up my large black medical bag and headed out to my truck. It had been a long, hot day, and what I wanted more than anything was a nice, cold beer. Drinking alone was depressing, so I shot a text over to Paris, asking if she wanted to meet me at the Elbow Room. She didn't answer right away, so I tossed my phone onto the passenger seat and headed in that direction.

Gripping the steering wheel of my old Ford pickup, I was relaxed, even though the cab bounced as it hit the tiniest potholes. Turning into the parking lot of the bar my brother Marcus owned, I hunted for a parking spot. I was happy to see the place packed. He'd steadily increased business since he bought it a few years ago. Pulling the heavy wood door, I wrinkled my nose. He had made a lot of changes, but had he been able to get rid of the stale cigarette smoke that seemed embedded into every inch of the place, it would have been even better.

Glancing at my phone one more time, I was shocked that Paris still hadn't replied. It was so unlike her, but then again, there was a baby in the house, so what did I really expect?

I headed for a seat at the bar, nodding to a few people I knew, and took the last open stool, the one tucked right against the wall.

"You look exhausted," my brother said, tapping his knuckles on the bar.

"Some days, I wonder why I decided to work with large animals." He set a pint of Yuengling in front of me without my having to order it, and I took a sip before continuing. "It's so damn hot outside. It would be much cushier in a clinic."

"True, but you'd be miserable, and you know it. How many times did Mom try to convince Dad to slow down or just open up a clinic?" Marcus rested his arms on the bar and made himself comfortable.

"I know . . . I just need to get used to the heat. Been in the classroom way too long."

"Too damn long." Marcus slapped the counter, making several people turn and stare at us. "Don't know how you did it. I sure as hell couldn't."

"I just knew that this was what I always wanted to do. I didn't consider anything else. There has been a Doctor Kinkaide taking care of people's animals in these parts since . . . well, the eighteen hundreds, with Dad's great-grandfather. It felt right to me." I took another swig from my bottle.

"Better you than me." Marcus laughed. "I know that we're only three years apart, but usually that kind of carry-on-family-tradition shit is put on the oldest son. I just wasn't cut out for school. I probably disappointed Dad."

"Stop. Where the fuck is that coming from? That is one thing neither of us was. You know better than that. Sure, Mom and Dad were in their fifties by the time they had me—"

Marcus interrupted. "Can you fucking imagine that?"

"No. I don't want to think about fifty-year-olds having sex, let alone fifty-year-olds who are our parents."

"Nothing like getting a student discount and a senior citizen discount at the same restaurant, huh?"

I picked up my beer and took another sip.

"Be right back. Need to actually act like the owner and check on the other patrons." Marcus stepped away.

Turning on the stool, I took in the crowd and smiled when I spotted Holland. She was talking to a few of her friends and rocking on the back two legs of her chair. I groaned, worrying that someone was going to come along and bump her and she'd tumble backward. But it seemed I didn't have to worry because she was leaning back to look to her left. I watched the youngest of the three Kelly sisters focus on her arch-nemesis and next-door neighbor. Unfortunately, their tables were fairly close together but not side by side, so everything they said still had to be shouted. Holland was . . . well, she had always been the hellion of the three. Just as I was getting up to go ask her if she knew where Paris was,

Holland stood so swiftly, the chair she'd been sitting in fell over.

"You are a sleezeball dirtbag dickhead of the worst degree. I have no clue why you moved here." Holland jabbed her index finger at the tall, extremely large man still sitting. "But you don't belong here. You might as well go back to that overpriced city you came from, Dick Brooks—"

"My name is Reid."

He was calm, which only aggravated Holland that much more. The two of them had been at each other's throats since he moved across the street from them. Most of the time, it was funny to watch because she would get irrationally angry and he would stay infuriatingly calm. One of these days, he was going to push her too far and she was going to burn his house to the ground.

She was one person whose bad side I wouldn't want to be on.

"Whatever, like I care." She snarled the words at him. "Your name will always be Dick to me."

Not wanting to be rude but deciding that this was no time for niceties, I made my way to her table and placed a hand on her shoulder. "Holland—"

"Get away from me, Asher. I'm pissed and don't want to say something to you that I will regret later. You are too nice. But this asshole"—Holland stepped around several people so she was close enough to poke Reid in the chest—"has insulted me for the last time."

I glanced back at the table where Holland had just been sitting. "How much have you had to drink?"

"Not a lot."

Reid raised one brow to challenge Holland's statement.

"Okay, fine. More than I had planned on, but still. It doesn't change the fact that this asshole insulted me."

"How did I insult you?" Reid smirked, not hiding his smile.

"You insulted the way I ride."

"I told you to watch your left leg because you tend to bring it in front of your body when you ride. I thought you'd like to know. We can't see ourselves riding, so we need other people to tell us what we can improve on. Sorry, next time, I'll just let you look like an idiot, you ungrateful brat."

"Brat? And what? You're all of a sudden the fuckin' horse-riding know-it-all?"

"Clearly, I know more than you since I know to keep my mouth shut and pay attention when someone is giving me helpful information."

"Helpful? That wasn't—"

"Okay. Enough." I held up my hands. "Stop it, Holland. Where are your keys?"

"In my pocket."

"Did you bring a purse?"

"Nooo."

My head felt like it was going to explode. "Come on. I'm taking you home." I grabbed her arm and glanced over to my brother, who was smirking. I wanted to punch him. Holland was like a little sister to us, so he could have helped me at any time.

I tossed him an ungrateful wave and then pulled my phone from my pocket. It was barely seven, and Paris still hadn't texted me back. At least she wasn't on her way here as I was walking out the door.

Holland was stewing in the passenger's seat; thankfully the Kelly ranch was just a few miles down State Road 46. The sign read Kelly Ranch and Iron Horse Stables, the only marker for their street, and as soon as I saw it, I flipped on my blinker. At one time that had been our school bus stop, and Paris and I had leaned against the beams while we waited.

I parked next to Paris's Jeep, which was parked up close to the house, and jumped out. I took two steps toward the front door and stopped.

I'd grown up in the woods, hell, I'd grown up right next to here, but the sound that stopped me wasn't a normal sound.

"Hehhhh." There it was again.

"Holland, stop."

"What?" She was still pissed.

"Hawp."

"Did someone say help?" Holland asked.

Turning around, I opened the door to my truck and reached under my seat. I slid out my lock box, where I kept my Dan Wesson six-inch .357—we lived in the country, after all. I didn't have much call to use it, but I was glad I had it.

"Help." Oh hell yes, that was definitely help.

Holland suddenly sounded less hostile as she moved to where I was standing on the driver's side.

"Stay here and call Braden. I'm going to go make sure Paris is okay."

"I'm going with you. Braden and London took Tera over to his parents'. They won't be home until late."

At the realization that Paris was here alone, all rationale escaped me. I headed to the house but stopped when I heard the plea again. It was coming from the side of the house. So, I made sure Holland was behind me, and together, we made our way slowly around to the side of the house.

"Paris, is that you?" I called out.

"Yaaaa."

I had no idea what was making that noise, but I hurried toward it anyway. Then I saw her. She was standing in the open doorway of the meat locker. She wasn't moving, but her glassy eyes kept glancing from me to something in front of her.

Lying across the walkway about three feet in front of her was the largest rattlesnake I'd ever seen.

No, I take that back, not just any rattlesnake, it was a motherfucking diamondback rattlesnake.

"Fuck." Already knowing I didn't have the right ammunition with me, I opened the chamber on my revolver and looked at the bullets just to be sure. I glanced over my shoulder to see Holland frozen a few feet behind me.

"Holland, I need you to do me a favor and go back to my truck get the snake-shot out of the glove box."

The rattler's tail lifted and shook at the ground vibrations from Holland's running feet.

"Kitten, listen to me. I know that you're freezing . . ." God, I felt so bad, she was shivering. "But I'm going to need you to move back into the freezer and away from the open door, okay?" I dumped the bullets, ready to fill once Holland returned.

Paris nodded.

"I'm going to get you out of there, don't worry. You know I won't leave you, right?"

Paris nodded again.

The snake coiled and lifted its head, but it lulled back and forth as it rattled its tail.

I turned at the sound of Holland's footsteps and grabbed the box. With shaking hands, I filled each of the six chambers and then turned back to the snake, which was still posed to strike.

"Is the snake drunk?" Holland whispered. "Or is it rabid?"

"Shhh." I waved Holland off. "Okay, sweetheart, move back." I closed the cylinder and took a few steps closer to the snake while Paris slid back a few steps.

I knew the snake was neither drunk nor rabid; it had

been caught off guard by the cold. He was alarmed by Paris and became defensive, which caused him to coil, but he'd been there so long, an early state of brumation had set in.

Bringing the gun up in front of me, I closed my less-dominant eye, and then focused. I fired, and the snake struck out, so I fired again and again and again until the thing stopped moving. Snake-shot was a capsule full of tiny pellets that sprayed in an arc to ensure a clean shot just in case the snake started to move, curl up, or flatten its body. Normally, I was all for letting animals go, but sometimes, you have to do what you have to do.

Once I was positive it wasn't going to somehow start moving again, I turned to search for a branch, broom, anything I could poke the damn snake with to make sure it was dead before getting too close.

"Here." Holland was bent over, huffing, trying to catch her breath as she held out a large hoe.

"Thanks." I took it from her and prodded the snake, which didn't move. "It's dead." I uncoiled the reptile, which was much larger than any I'd seen before. Once it was spread out, I counted the buttons. There were thirteen. This was a serious-sized snake.

But it was dead, so I shifted it off the walkway and turned to Paris, who still hadn't come out.

She was sitting on the cold concrete floor, curled into a tight ball. Racked with worry for this woman who I'd been in love with my whole life, I gazed into her chocolate eyes. "Oh, Kitten." Then I lowered my mouth to hers, and in that moment, she acquiesced, giving in to this undeniable bond we had. It wasn't deep or wild. It was soft and reassuring. It was something we both needed—she needed to know she'd been rescued, and I needed to know she was safe. "Come on. Put your arms around me." I lifted her and carried her out of their meat freezer. Holland locked up behind me then followed me into their house. "Will you put some coffee on for your sister?" I asked before heading down the hall that led to Paris's bedroom and straight to her bathroom, where I set her onto the counter. Removing her shoes and socks, I turned on the faucet and let the water turn warm before moving to the tub and filling it with hot water as well. I wanted to fill the small room with steam and help warm her without shocking her system.

"Yo-you . . . you sho-showed up." Paris's teeth were chattering.

"I sent you a text, and when you didn't reply, I got worried."

"I . . . I left my phone inside."

I grabbed a towel and dampened it with the warm water, then wrapped it around her feet before pulling her hands into mine and warming them with my breath—anything to infuse her with my body heat. God, she felt like ice. But I didn't see any frostbite.

"Wha-wha-what time is it?"

Not wanting to let go of her hands, I hazarded a guess. "Probably close to eight."

"Oh."

"What time did you go out there?"

Paris shivered. "Jus . . . just after lunch. I just ran in to g-gr-grab some beef because our house freezer was getting low, and we just g-got an Angus back from the butcher." Paris took several deep breaths, trying to let the steam in the room warm her from the inside.

I was glad to hear her talking even though she was shivering, but she didn't seem to have any memory loss, and since the door was open, I seriously doubted hypothermia, but I wasn't taking any chances, not with my Paris.

"But when I was going to leave, I saw him. He w-wa-was . . . coiled like he was going to attack. So I stepped back and

31

waited." She sat there, as if trying to compose her thoughts. "I couldn't close the door since it swings out, and I couldn't reach it, plus then I'd be frozen to death. But the damn thing wouldn't move. I made noises. I figured he wouldn't come into the freezer. You know, cold-blooded and all."

"You probably scared him, so he settled in, ready to fight, but the cold air got to him. Cold air slows snakes down until they finally go to sleep. That was probably why he didn't move on, he was too tired."

"But he kept shaking that damn tail."

"Well, he still felt threatened. He wasn't going to let you out."

A shiver wracked her body, but this time it wasn't from the cold. "I hate snakes. I don't even like snakeskin boots."

"Don't worry, I'll make sure he's gone before you go back out there. You won't have to see it again."

Just then, Holland came in with an oversized cup of coffee. "Here, sip slowly. This will warm you from the inside."

Holland moved and turned off the tub and sink faucets since the room was full of steam. "I turned the air conditioner off in your room but left a fan on just to circulate air. I wanted to get the chill off."

"Thanks, Holland." She gave me a worried smile. "She's going to be fine, I promise." Turning my attention back to Paris, I asked, "How you feeling?"

"Better," Paris mumbled as she held on to the mug of coffee.

"Let me look at your toes." I unwrapped the towels and was pleased that everything looked fine. There was no dull discoloration to her skin. "Do you want to sit in a warm bath?"

Paris shook her head. "I want to lie down."

"I don't want you to go to sleep yet. I need to make sure that your internal temperature is back to normal, okay?"

"Will you stay?" She had no clue what she was asking of me. I'd do anything this girl asked of me. I wanted to stay. I wanted to stay every night for the rest of my life with her.

"Of course, but let's get some food into you before you get settled."

"Okay." Paris placed an icy-cold hand on my arm.

ASHER

*P*aris's room was the epitome of girly. It was
everything that represented females, from the
white bedspread to the pillows. Not pillows you could sleep
on or stack behind you to make yourself comfortable. No,
these were worthless pillows that did nothing but take up
room. She removed them, set them carefully aside each
evening, then organized them perfectly each morning. I
swore to god, it was the stupidest thing I'd ever seen, and one
of the many things that made women endearing. Though,
when I was the one moving them all, it wasn't quite so cute.

"I'll be right back. I'm going to go see if I can find Holland
or if I can hunt for something to eat," I said after she had
settled under the covers, still clutching the mug of coffee. I
pulled the door open and then stepped aside just in time to
avoid being knocked over by London. Braden was following
behind her, with his daughter tucked close to his chest.

"Oh my god, are you okay? I'm so sorry that no one was
here. What can I get you?" I stared at the woman who I'd
known since the day I was born and was shocked. London

35

had never been the mothering sort—that was always Paris—but holy shit, she sounded like a mom.

"I'm fine now that I'm warm. I just want to rest."

"Holland told us what happened. Daddy kept talking about putting a phone in there. He was always afraid of one of us getting locked in. That was when he changed the door so it was single-chambered and you could only keep outsiders from getting in, not people inside from getting out."

"Stop, don't overreact. What were the odds of a damn snake taking up residency in front of the door? Well, up until now I'd say never, but that theory was just blown out of the fucking water. Besides, we use our cell phones so much, if we did have a land line, I wouldn't remember a damn number to be able to call anyone."

"You could always call 9-1-1," Braden, the ever-helpful sheriff's deputy, offered.

"But what about Tera? What about when she starts running around?" London was already frantic with worry.

"Calm down. We'll get some snake repellent. But truthfully, snakes aren't pack animals," Braden said, trying to calm his wife.

"I know that, but Paris is freaked, and she is all that matters right now. If snake repellant makes her feel comfortable, then, damn it, we will put that stuff everywhere." I met Braden's eyes, because although London was claiming that this was for Paris, truthfully, she was the only one on the edge of hysteria. But I bit my tongue.

"Okay, okay. London, we'll figure out something."

London's wide eyes whipped from me back to her sister. It was actually kind of sweet that London was wringing her hands so hard her knuckles were turning white, a mothering gesture that I'd never imagined seeing from her. "How about if I go make something to eat?" London asked. "What do you want? Just tell me, I'll make anything."

Paris chuckled. "Y'all are exhausting me. Besides, I'm not very hungry. I'll eat something later."

Paris was the one who always did the cooking, canning, and kept the ranch house running. Which for the first time was going to be a problem, since I wasn't sure if anyone else actually knew how to cook.

"Okay, just let me know when you're ready, and I'll get you something. Braden, you'll let me know, won't you?" London asked as she strolled toward the door, stopping to place a peck on her husband's lips and then her daughter's head.

"Of course."

"You need anything, Paris?" Braden asked before following his wife out.

"No, I'm good." Paris shook her head, chills still racking her body. "Thanks, though." Braden left and closed the door behind him.

"Why don't we get you into something warm?" I pulled out a pair of socks from her top left dresser drawer. I knew where she kept those. I couldn't count the number of times she had begged me to get her a pair of socks while I was over late and we were in her living room watching movies. The woman had the coldest feet, and I was a sucker to please her. But that was the only drawer I'd ever been in. I'd never been nosey. "I have no clue where you keep your pajamas."

"Next drawer down. I have a blue flannel fleece set at the bottom. It's super warm."

Digging down, I tried to ignore the silk nightgowns, but my imagination was off to some distant corner of a world where I could see Paris in these. I pulled out the set she asked for and handed it to her. "Here you go. I'll be right outside the door." I stared at her for just a moment, this woman I'd fallen in love with sometime over the last twenty-nine years of my life. Reaching forward, I trailed a thumb across her cheek, and she curled in toward my hand like a cat trying to encourage petting.

"God, your hands feel so good, so warm."

I was going to pass out, right here. My head felt faint, and my pants suddenly felt too tight . . . right in the crotch. I needed to get out of there before she looked down and saw my growing erection. I was as bad as some fourteen-year-old, all because of her sigh, her moan. And the feel of her velvety-smooth skin, which was still cold to the touch and a stark contrast to mine, had me on fire.

"Hurry, I'll be in the hall." Rushing to the door, I closed it as I stepped out of the room. When I was safely out in the hallway, I rested my head against the wall, closed my eyes, and tried to get everything under control. I'd never been so afraid as I was seeing that rattlesnake and then realizing she was blocked. Fucking worried about her, worried about how long she'd been in the freezer, worried about the possibility of losing her to something like a snake bite. Paris and I had been playing this game long enough, and I knew I just needed to come out and tell her how I felt.

I blew out a deep breath and looked at the picture hanging on the wall across from me. It was of the first year I decided that I was too big to dress up for Halloween, but Paris still wanted to dress up. I smiled at the memory and moved to the next photo, it was from a school play, I could remember exactly which one, maybe first or second grade. She was so damn cute. Fuck, what was her name in that play . . . oh, Mrs. Wishy Washy.

I had just moved to the third photo when she called me. "Okay, you can come in."

When I opened the door, I was stunned, my breath was taken away, not because of what she was wearing, but because of the girl herself. My Paris in plain old pajamas with a smile on her face, despite the hell she had just been through.

"Get into bed." I moved next to her bed and pulled back the covers so she could crawl back under them. Then I waited for her to right herself and prop her back against the headboard before I pulled the covers back up and tucked them around her.

I took two steps toward the chair she kept in the corner of her room before she stopped me. "Come over here with me." Paris patted the bed.

"I can sit in the chair."

"No, please, I want you with me. I need your body heat."

God, did she not know what she was doing to me? I was stretched tighter than a fucking drum. Rolling my neck back and forth, I straightened my shoulders and then crawled next to her but stayed on top of the covers.

Fuck, this wasn't such a great idea because she could see how hard my dick was, all because of her.

"I was so scared, Asher. I had no clue if you were going to find me. I didn't know when London or Holland would be home. I was afraid I was going to freeze to death."

I sat up, turned to position myself, and faced her. Reaching forward, I gripped Paris's shoulders. "Don't you get it? I'll always be here for you. I will always find you."

"Yeah, but how was I supposed to know that? You weren't supposed to be coming by, Holland was out, and London was at her in-laws. I really had no clue what I would have done had you not shown up."

"Well, I did, so that's all that matters. But don't ever leave the house without your cell phone again, okay?"

"I was just running out to the freezer. I go out there all the time."

"But considering everything that happened last year,

everything with Ryan, I figured you'd be a little more cautious."

"Ryan's in jail. Plus, he wanted London, not me."

I shook my head, because she wasn't getting the point. Last year, their long-time ranch-hand became obsessed with London after she started dating Braden. "I would've thought that just watching what London went through would be enough to scare the shit out of you. Don't go anywhere, not even to the mailbox without a phone. Promise me, Paris. I don't know what I'd do if anything happened to you. Promise me."

"Okay, I promise."

Satisfied with her answer, I leaned back and made myself comfortable, letting Paris curl up next to me. Holding her in my arms, I trailed my fingers up and down, watching the tiny goosebumps appear like ripples in the waves.

"Paris, can I talk to you about something?"

"Of course."

"It's been on my mind for a long time, but after today, I think I need to lay it all out there. The thought of losing you, I can't handle it." I felt my heart pick up its pace and my fingers stuttered in the journey over her skin. "We're best friends, but I think we could be more than that. I think I've always known, but the first time I felt it, we were in middle school—"

"Asher, don't do this . . ."

"Why not? I'm in love with you, and I'm pretty sure you're in love with me."

Paris shook her head, holding her hand up against her mouth.

"Paris, I'm in love with you. I've been in love with you for as long as I can remember. You're everything I've ever wanted. We are meant to be together. Haven't you ever wondered why you've never found anyone? Or, hell, why I never found anyone? It isn't because the person I'm supposed to be with is out there somewhere. It's because the person I am supposed to be with has been right in front of me all along. It's always been you for me. I love you so fucking much."

"Why are you doing this? I can't. I can't lose you."

"What are you talking about? You won't lose me. We've been together our entire lives. I don't have a single memory that doesn't involve you. How do you not see this, Paris? Prom? It was us. Graduation? Us. First kiss? That was us too. My college graduation? You and me. Everything has been about us. A team. I thought you were seeing it too."

"There is no us. I don't know what you're talking about. We're just friends."

"You don't mean that. I know you feel something more."

"We're friends. That's all. Best friends, but best friends aren't lovers. You goof off with your best friend, you joke with your best friend, but just because you're best friends with someone, that doesn't automatically mean you're going to marry them."

"I know that, but you and me? We're different. No one would have a stronger relationship than we would." I wanted to shake her. Reach up and grab her perfect damn shoulders and just shake some sense into her.

"But what if it doesn't work out? I'd lose everything. I'd lose you."

She didn't get it. I was offering her all of myself, and she was too worried about the what-ifs to see it. "You won't lose me, you would never lose me, Paris. I'm in love with you. You can't tell me that you didn't know it."

"Stop saying that. You may love me, but you aren't in love with me, Asher. Maybe you're in love with the idea of being in love and I'm just convenient, but friends can't be lovers. I refuse to throw away a lifetime of friendship because you can't tell the difference."

"I'm pretty sure I know exactly how I feel, but tell me about why you think it wouldn't work, why you won't even give us a shot."

"My parents had been friends before they got married, and look how that ended. Divorce. My dad died with a broken heart, and I have no clue where my mother is."

"Don't you get it? Your parents' relationship was not the end-all, be-all of relationships, and you shouldn't use it as a status quo. My parents were friends, and look at them, they were married more than fifty years. Wake up and look around. You are taking one failure and making that the bar by which you measure all relationships. It isn't fair. God, if your mom were here right now, I'd be tempted to hit her just for planting those things in your head, and I've never hit a woman. But damn it, Paris, you're being ridiculous. You've deluded yourself into thinking that love is supposed to be a certain way. Well, it isn't, it's different for each person, each couple."

Paris let out a heart-wrenching sob. "I'm more like my mom than you know, than obviously your mom knows."

"You aren't anything like her." I was fighting to control my temper.

"I'm such a jealous person. I'm so jealous of everyone. God, I love my sister, she means everything to me, but I'm having such a hard time being around her. She has every-thing I want. I'm so jealous that she has it when she's the one who never wanted it."

"That doesn't mean you're like your mom. That means you want *to be* a mom. You want babies. You'll be a fabulous mother and a wonderful wife. You love me, Paris, I know you do, I feel it."

Paris adamantly shook her head. "I don't know. Maybe I was wrong, maybe I don't want kids."

"Paris, stop. Yes, you do, you've always wanted children. You can have them—hell, you can have anything you've ever wanted. All you need to do is find the guts to go after it. To take off the damn blinders and see that everything you've ever wanted is right here in front of you."

"No, Asher. You're my best friend. I feel safe with you. But that isn't enough." Tears were streaming down her face, but I no longer cared if she cried or not. "I love you, I'm not in love with you. There's a big difference. I want that burning passion that a couple in love is supposed to have. We're just friends, and we'll only ever be friends."

I stood, fighting not to say something that I would regret later. Fuck that, I could do with a little regret in my life. "Maybe you're right." Paris stared at me, eyes red and swollen as she waited for me to finish my sentence. "Maybe you are just like your mom. Too stubborn and too afraid to keep something you don't deserve."

Paris let out a whoosh of air, and I didn't care if my words hurt her. I was too busy thinking of how I was going to pull out the knife she'd jammed into my heart.

PARIS

*S*aturday

    My alarm went off at five the next morning. Stretching to reach the buzzer, I groaned as my muscles finally made themselves and everything they'd been through yesterday known. I couldn't remember my legs ever being so sore, but then again, I couldn't remember a time when I ever had to stand at attention for so long. It was probably a combination of the fear, the cold, and the stress.

Rolling back over, I pulled a pillow on top of my head and tried to forget the anger that had been on Asher's face yesterday. The hurt that had crossed every inch of his once-upon-a-time smile.

What he had proposed was ridiculous and completely out of the blue. I knew that it had changed our friendship irrevocably, that by wanting to preserve our friendship, I had ruined it.

That he had ruined it by saying those things.

By not understanding.

I felt the first tears starting to bubble up inside of me again. This time, I let them fall, soaking my pillowcase,

45

exhausting my worn-out mind to go with my exhausted body.

* * *

SUNDAY

Someone opened my bedroom door, but I couldn't be bothered enough to open my eyes or demand they go away.

"Paris, honey, you want something to eat?" London asked. I didn't want to see anyone, talk to anyone, or do anything. And I most certainly didn't want to eat.

"No."

"I'm going to call the doctor, okay?"

"No. Just leave me alone."

"I can't, I'm worried about you."

"Don't. Go away. You have your own family. You have a husband and baby. Just go, leave me alone. Go. Get out, leave me alone!" I continued raising my voice until I heard the door shut.

No one understood what I was going through; they didn't get it. Asher had been the closest thing I had to . . . a brother. No, that wasn't right. The closest thing to a husband . . . no. That wasn't right either. I didn't know what he had been, other than my best friend, and I'd lost him, which made it feel as if a small part of me had died.

* * *

MONDAY

"Okay, time to get up. Enough. Not sure what's going on, but you need to let us help you." London's voice was piercing. I wasn't sure whether to muffle my ears or cover my eyes from the bright sun peering in through the windows.

"Close those curtains."

"Nope. It looks like a freaking mausoleum in here." London's chirpy voice was really getting on my fucking nerves.

"Ugh," I groaned as Holland pulled back my covers, exposing me to the cool, conditioned air before hopping onto the middle of my bed.

"I brought you some coffee and toast. You haven't eaten in three days."

Fine. Maybe if I did what they wanted, they would leave me alone again. I pushed up to sitting and took the plate Holland offered.

"What's going on? This has to be more than being scared by a snake. We haven't seen Asher in days. Did you and he have a fight?" London asked as she sat next to Holland.

I took a bite, and I swore to god it took me forever to get it down because I had a lump right in the middle of my throat. "I don't think Asher's ever going to talk to me again."

"Why? What happened?" London's voice softened.

"He told me that he loves me."

"Why are you crying about that? Of course he loves you. That man has loved you all his life. We all could see it."

"Because I told him that I don't feel the same way about him."

"You what?" Holland jumped up, her voice rising. "Are you an idiot?"

"Calm down, Holland, let Paris explain." London tugged on Holland's arm and pulled her back to the bed. "Is there someone else?"

"No." I shook my head, tears splashing. "Not yet, at least, but I want there to be. I want someone who sweeps me off my feet. I want that burning desire that you see in movies. I don't feel that for Asher."

"Paris, that is the most ridiculously naive thing I've ever heard. You have no clue what burning passion feels like, yet

47

you are assuming you can't have that with Asher without even trying. You're so blind that you can't even see what's in front of your face."

London's words might as well have been a whip, the way they lashed out against me.

"Leave me alone. I want to go back to sleep. I take care of you guys every day. I have for my entire fucking life, can I not have one week to just be tired?"

"I think that's the most selfish thing I've ever heard come out of your mouth."

"Well, just goes to show how little you know me. I'm a very selfish, self-centered person. You would hate me if you knew the thoughts inside my head, just like Asher hates me."

"I could never hate you. And I don't—not for one second —believe that Asher hates you. He may be mad or hurt, but the man could never hate you."

For years, I'd replayed my mother's words in my head and had held them like the gospel, pulling tidbits here and there when I needed a little assurance that I was making the right choices. "Do you know that I heard everything she and Dad said the night she left?"

"You did? Why didn't you ever tell me?" London looked hurt.

"What did they say?" Holland scooted closer, finally paying attention.

"Mom and Dad had been friends before they got married, and that was what ruined their marriage, they didn't have the romance. I don't want Asher and me to end up like Dad and Mom." My voice was almost a broken whisper. "I couldn't live with myself if I hurt Asher, he's the kindest man I know."

"Paris Jean Kelly, you are not Mom. God, I wish you could hear yourself." London looked more pissed than concerned. "None of us knows how good of friends they were before they got married, but I have seen you and Asher, watched you two together all of your lives. And when Asher went away to college, it was as if you were lost without him. When you found out he was coming home, you turned into a totally different person. When something is wrong, Asher is the person you call. He's the person you trust, and I can't believe you're so unwilling to admit that to yourself."

"And what is that?"

"That Asher is your soulmate. You are giving up something that is fated because of what some crazy woman who abandoned her children and husband said. You're using Mom's excuse for leaving Dad to keep from admitting that you're in love with Asher—"

"I'm not."

"Whatever." London waved her hand, totally dismissing me. "So, what was Mom's excuse for leaving her three little girls? Can't say that we were her friends. Are you going to use that same excuse and abandon your children?"

"Never. I'd never leave my kids."

"Then why are you sitting here claiming to be anything like Cora Lee Kelly?"

Holland stood, glaring. "You are even more stupid than I thought. Damn. I can't be here for this."

I flinched as she slammed the door behind her.

"Sounds to me like you're just making excuses to cover up for your fears. It's been pathetic watching you two all these years. If you don't recognize the mistake you are making for what it is, then I guess there isn't much else I can say." London rose and moved to my bedroom door. "There is breakfast in the kitchen, help yourself. I'm going to get Tera and take her out for some fresh air. I think that I need some as well."

I waited until London shut my door before getting up and dragging myself off to my bathroom, because I smelled terrible. It took me almost an hour to get myself ready and out to the kitchen. It was the first time I'd been out there since Friday, when I'd decided to go to the meat locker.

I smiled when I saw a large package of beef tips wrapped in brown paper from the butcher sitting in the fridge. That someone had taken time to grab food from the outdoor freezer and finish the job that I didn't, as well as set some out to defrost, settled something in me. This was all going to work out. It had to. Asher was going to realize I was right, and he'd start coming back over, he had to.

There was no harm in being the first to cross that invisible divide between us, so I grabbed my phone and shot him a quick text.

ME: I'm getting ready to start lunch. I hope you stop by.

I'D NEVER HAD to initiate a text conversation with Asher before. He was always just here. Breakfast, lunch, and most dinners, I could always count on Asher at our house.

I smiled when I saw three bubbles appear. It was weird that something that said nothing would make me so happy. Well . . . that was, until the text came through.

ASHER: Thanks for the invitation, but I can't. Busy.
    Me: Oh. Then maybe dinner.
    Asher: Not tonight. I'm meeting Marcus.
    Me: I miss you.
    Asher: I miss you too.

HOW COULD four words hurt so much? *I miss you too.* But they did. I stared at the last text, praying that another would follow, one more where he'd say he changed his mind and would come over.

I watched for the bubbles, prayed, my heart picking up speed then plummeting with the realization that none would appear.

* * *

BY FRIDAY, I was lost. I'd been sending Asher text messages every day, and he always had some excuse for not being able to come by.

I was hurt. I kept telling myself that the hurt was over losing a friend and nothing else. I was clearing away the dinner dishes when London walked in holding Tera.

"Hey, do you mind watching her while Braden and I move all this stuff over to our house?"

"Of course not." I grabbed the small speaker for the monitor and clipped it to my jeans as she laid Tera in the bassinet. "You sure you don't want me to do that instead? You could stay here."

"No, I'm fine. It'll do me some good. Besides, it'll do Braden some good. The man is going crazy. This no sex for six weeks . . . you'd think he'd been sentenced to death, the way he's acting."

I held up my hands in protest. "No. Stop right there. You have a tendency to overshare. I don't want to know any more."

London let out an evil laugh. "You mean you don't want to hear what I did last night to alleviate . . ."

"Nooo. Shut up. Ooo, gross. You're my sister, but worse than that is Braden. I'm sorry, but I look at him like a brother."

London winked. "Thank god I don't see him as a brother. I'm pretty sure the things we've been doing are illegal in at least twenty countries, and probably some states."

"Go." I pointed to the door and then returned to the dishes, but as soon as London left, I hightailed it to Tera and lifted her into my arms. We settled into the rocking chair, and I held her while she slept. Someday there would be a man who I would be willing to do anything for just to have a few moments alone with them. Someday, Tera, someday I was going to be someone's girl.

The knock at the front door had me heaving myself up with Tera still in my arms and then gently laying her back down in her cradle.

When I finally made it through the house again and to the front door, my damn hands were sweating, and I was praying it was Asher while also hoping it wasn't. If it was Asher and he felt he needed to knock instead of walk right in, then it was just another reminder that our friendship was truly over.

But it wasn't Asher.

In fact, it wasn't anyone I recognized, yet, I knew that I knew her. She was me—well, me in thirty years.

"Mom?" The single word cracked as it passed my lips. It was such an unfamiliar word.

"I can't tell you how happy it makes me to know that you remember me." I glanced down at her hands gripping her purse. She had acrylic nails. No one out here had fake nails. They were impractical. I couldn't very well grip Ursula's reins tight if I couldn't even make a fist because my nails were so damn long.

Lost in thought, I stood there staring at her, not sure what to do. Was I supposed to invite her in or slam the door in her face?

"What are you doing here?"

"I've missed you three so much. Plus, I heard that I'm a grandmother, and I can't wait to see the baby."

"Ummm." Okay, words weren't coming to me. I had no clue what to say or do. I needed to call London.

"Aren't you going to invite me in? I'm tired, I've been traveling for hours to come see you girls."

"Yeah, sure. Won't you have a seat?" I stepped back, pointed to the sofa, and allowed my mother, Cora Kelly, to walk into the home she hadn't stepped foot in since I was seven years old.

"This place hasn't changed one bit, it still feels like home to me."

Home? Whose home? Not her home, I wanted to say but didn't. I watched her as she moved around the large room. All I could think of were the number of times I'd imagined her returning, and suddenly, the feeling seemed to be crushing. All the birthday, holidays, even my high-school graduation, I had wished for her to be here, and she had missed them all.

"So, it took a baby to get you to come see us?"

"Well, that and I just heard about your father . . . I'm so sorry. He was a good man."

"Yes, he was. He did a lot for us."

"Where are your sisters? Where's the baby?" Cora asked.

Looking at her was like looking into a mirror . . . one I wished I could shatter. Our hair was the same shade, one a poet might call the color of honey, but I called dishwater. Our eyes were what a romanticist would wax on about being similar to dark chocolate, but truthfully, they were the same color as manure. Our height, our body shape, probably even our shoe sizes were almost identical. The only difference was that she had wrinkles.

"The baby is sleeping. Why don't you have a seat, I'll go fix us some iced tea and I'll send a text to Holland and London."

"Okay, thank you, Paris."

Walking into the kitchen, I pulled out my phone and scrolled to my group message.

Me: HOLY SHIT, Cora is here.

London: Cora? As in our mother?

Me: Yep, that's the only Cora I know.

London: WTF?

Holland: I'm on my way.

Me: Hurry please. She wants to see Tera.

London: Ah, fuck no, don't let her anywhere near my baby. You hear me?

Me: Okay. I would never. Calm down.

I PUT the phone down and grabbed glasses and tea before starting a pot of coffee and calling Cora into the kitchen with me.

I'd just set out the sugar and cream when the front door flew open and Holland ran in. She halted in the archway to the kitchen and stared at the woman sitting in what once was Daddy's chair. None of us sat there, but I didn't stop her when she'd chosen that spot. Before Holland could say a word, London came in, Braden close behind her. I fought to hold back my smile as I heard him whispering to her, "Stay calm, London. Let's just think this through. I'm here with you, honey."

But London was obviously having none of Braden's soothing words. "What's she doing in Dad's chair? There are seven more around the table for her to choose from."

"London—" I snapped.

"Oh, I'm sorry. I'll move." Cora slid one seat over, bringing her coffee with her. "You three look beautiful. I've missed you so much."

"Cut the bullshit. What do you want? We haven't seen you in almost twenty-two years, so you can't tell me that you all of a sudden missed us." London's words were harsh, but she'd been the one most affected by Mom's leaving. London had been ten and took it personally.

"I just heard about your dad. I was so sorry to hear it. That's when I heard you had a baby as well."

"Where?" London glared at me like it was my fault that Cora knew all of this.

"Where what?" Cora looked from Holland, to London, to me.

"Where did you hear the latest news about us?"

"Have a seat, and I'll tell you everything."

Braden moved and pulled out a chair for his wife, then held out a chair for Holland and me before taking a seat next to London.

"Your dad and I always stayed in touch. I thought about you girls often, so I used to write to him and ask him to send me pictures. Every now and then, he would, usually on your birthdays. Well, I hadn't heard from him in a while, so I decided to try to contact Wally. He and your dad were always so close. He told me about your dad passing away and then about London getting married and having a baby. I knew that I had to come see you all. It sounds bad, I know. But with your dad gone, I could finally see you. He wouldn't let me see you before. He used to return all of the letters I would write you three."

"That doesn't make sense, he didn't want you to leave in the first place. Maybe when we were younger he was trying to protect us, but not once we were older." I looked to my sisters for their thoughts.

"She's right. That doesn't make sense," Holland agreed. "Dad was all about family."

"I don't believe it," London murmured, crossing her arms

and totally blocking off anything Cora had to say. London looked at me and then at Holland. "If Wally told her about us, then he needs to go. He has no business talking about us, especially to her. After all the bullshit last year, I would think he would know that." London pushed back from the table.

But I couldn't blame her for being angry. Wally had endangered all of us and is lucky we forgave him in the first place. It was his misguided love for someone who he'd thought was his son that left him open to the manipulation of a man who ended up assaulting London.

Although I didn't see anything wrong with Wally telling Cora the obvious facts that were clearly public record and not gossip, I understood London's point, and I'd always be on my sister's side.

ASHER

I'd been working on drowning what was left of my heart for the better part of a week.

"Hey, Asher, why do you look so sad? Care if I sit?"

Glancing up, I was nearly poked in the eyes by boobs. Unfortunately, they were boobs I'd seen before. Well, boobs that many of us had seen before. "Hello, Etta. I'd like to be alone if you don't mind."

"Don't be like that, Asher. Where's your tagalong?" Her words were meant to be a barb to Paris, which was both unwelcome and infuriating. I refused to let her know anything or think anything bad about Paris.

"She's at home. Her sister just had a baby, so it's kind of hectic around the house."

"Well, since you're here all alone, why don't you dance with me?"

"I don't feel like dancing."

"Oh, come on. Please?" Etta pouted.

Did girls not realize that there was absolutely nothing sexy about looking like a fucking duck? I looked to my brother, silently urging him to save me from this nightmare. Thankfully, he did.

"Hey, Etta, if you don't mind, my brother and I have some shit we need to talk about." Marcus set the beer in front of me and then slid into the chair opposite me.

"Suit yourself. You know where I'll be." Etta rubbed her fingers down the side of my cheek. I reached up and grabbed her hand and pushed it back toward her.

Etta was blonde with blue eyes, and her breasts were clearly as fake as her personality. She was everything Paris wasn't.

Fuck.

Why couldn't I stop thinking about Paris?

"You look like you've just been hit by a Mack truck," Marcus said as he took a swig from his own mug of beer.

"That good, huh?"

"Was it something Etta said, or are you and Paris still on the outs?"

I cocked one eyebrow and stared at him over the rim of my drink. "Paris. I'm fucking delusional. All this time I thought that we were working toward something. Fuck, I even asked Sam if I could marry her one day."

"You did?" Marcus choked on his drink as it went down the wrong pipe, obviously shocked by my statement.

"I did. I knew he wouldn't be around for me to ask him when it was really time, so I had a talk with him when he was in hospice. He gave me his blessing; he said he knew it would always be Paris and me." I took a long swallow. "Why doesn't she fucking see it? She's so goddamned blind. I'm good enough to fill in when she needs a date, wants to go out— hell, even when she wants to kiss someone. But I'm not good enough for her to date. We're done."

"I don't believe that for one second. Give her time. I've never been able to figure her out. London was easy because she was so methodical. She was a rules kind of girl. Holland is all fire and runs based on emotions. But Paris? I don't know . . ." Marcus shook his head as he tried to figure it out.

"Heart. Paris rules with her heart."

"Maybe that's it, and since I no longer have a heart thanks to Maria . . ."

"The bitch," we both said in unison.

"I guess that's why I don't understand Paris."

A few years ago, Marcus had fallen in love with a girl who seemed sweet at first, but then, almost overnight, she decided that she wanted more, that he wasn't giving her enough. I was not sure exactly what he wasn't giving her enough of, because he gave her everything. Fact was, the girl was immature, self-centered, and was only interested in Marcus as long as he gave her gifts. When money was tight because he was opening the bar, she was ready to move on.

"I'm sorry, Ash. It will get better." Marcus raised his mug and held it out to me in a moment of brotherly solidarity. We silently toasted.

"Thanks. I'll be fine. I need to wrap my head around the idea that the only woman I've ever loved rejected me. I've spent almost thirty years being in love with her, and when I finally tell her, she says, 'Nah, I don't feel the same.'"

Marcus lifted his head and saw something over by the bar. "I'll be right back. Jett needs something."

"Bring me back another one, will you?" Marcus nodded and then headed to the bar. Jett had been working for Marcus since just after he opened. He made great drinks but was shitty at customer relations.

I dwelled on all things Paris as I finished my beer and then smiled when another was slid in front of me.

"From your brother." Jett smiled and then headed back behind the bar.

"Thanks."

Sometime between me sitting at the table and this moment, the bar had gotten crowded. Sure, the place was always busy, but on weekends it was slammed thanks to dollar drafts and the house band Marcus had brought in. He'd even moved the pool tables and old pinball machines from the middle of the bar to the back, so he could add a small stage and a dance floor.

Most of the people here were regulars, but there was one girl standing by the far wall, her shoulder propped against it, who wasn't. Something in her eyes mirrored my own. They were sad, lost, as if she were longing to drown away the feelings.

I watched her, her head slightly swayed, her toe tapped, and it wasn't until she brought her hand up to wipe away a tear that I realized she was crying while singing to the song.

I wasn't sure why—and probably wouldn't ever be able to explain what came over me—but I waved until I caught her attention. Signaling to the chair opposite me, I invited her to sit.

She took a few steps and then halted, then took a few more until she was standing next to me.

"You're welcome to sit. You look like you have a lot on your mind. I'm not hitting on you, in fact, I'm fine drinking alone. But if you feel anything like I do, then misery loves company."

She took a seat and stared up at the stage. "Girl problems?" she asked without looking in my direction.

"Something like that."

"Guy problems?"

I coughed. "No. Girl, but only one problem."

"And that would be?" She waited for me to answer, but I didn't know this woman, and I didn't feel like spilling my heart to some stranger. "I'm Ellie, by the way. My husband just left me."

"Ouch. I'm sorry to hear that."

"For the best man at our wedding."

I spat my drink out at her words. "What?"

"Yeah. Apparently, the Irish Catholics frown on that sort of thing, so he hid it. I came home early from work and thought he was upstairs with another woman, which was so cliché it was almost funny. Then I opened the bedroom door to discover that it wasn't a woman he was cheating on me with, but his best friend."

"Is that why you were crying? Sorry, I couldn't help noticing."

She absently wiped at her face. "Yes and no. I mean, yes, because it's sad, you know. I mean, when I married him, I hoped it would be forever. I wanted a family and the happily ever after. But no, because I'm happy for him, I really am. I'm glad he found his true love. I just wish he wouldn't have dragged me through the entire ordeal. It's like he punished me because he wasn't brave enough to come out of the closet. What did I ever do to him except love him?"

I waved to the bar and caught Marcus's attention and signaled for two. "Beer okay?"

"Yeah, that sounds great. I'm sorry, I promise not to keep moaning on."

Jett delivered them and then left us.

"I'm Asher, and I told the woman that I've been in love with almost my entire life how I felt and she shot me down."

"Were you two dating?"

"No, but we've been best friends since we were born. We were each other's first kiss—not because it was romantic, but because we were curious. We went to prom together. I've known that she was the one since seventh grade. I thought she felt the same way."

"Girls are so stupid."

61

"Tell me about it." We sat in silence for a few moments and drank our beer.

"So, how do you get such great service here?"

"See that guy behind the bar?"

She turned and looked. "Yeah, he sort of looks like you."

"He should. We're brothers, and he owns the place."

"Oh, that's Marcus?" The woman looked back over toward him again. "Then you must be the veterinarian."

"Yeah, how'd you know?"

"My brother told me. After everything that happened with Lance—"

I choked on my beer and then coughed. "*Lance*? That didn't give it away?"

"Shut up. Anyway, after everything that happened with Lance, my brother convinced me to move here and stay with him. He just bought a large horse ranch. He raises thoroughbreds."

"Wait. Is your brother Reid Brooks?"

"Yep."

"Then we're practically neighbors. The Kelly ranch is in between my family's land and your brother's. Well, since it seems that Reid told you about us, what is it that you do?"

"It's funny you should ask. I'm a vet tech, but I have a love for horses, so if you need someone, I'm your girl." Ellie patted her chest for emphasis.

"Believe me, I wish I could hire you, but I'm just starting out. This is only my second year. It will probably be another year before I'm ready to hire anyone."

"The last place I worked, I was a volunteer. Money is one thing I've always had. If you could use the help, I'd love to get out of the house and work with the animals. I miss it. Back in Kentucky, there were a lot of rescue shelters that had an in-house veterinarian. You all don't do that here."

"No, they call me, or someone mobile like me, to do the work."

"Well, think about it. I'd love to help." Ellie was smiling bright with excitement.

"Nothing to think about, you want the work, you got it." With Ellie helping, I could take on more clients. Adding more to my already packed work load had never sounded enticing until now . . . anything to keep my mind off the one woman who occupied every corner of it. "Can you start on Monday?"

"Absolutely. It will give me plenty of time to get drunk tonight and still nurse the hangover." Ellie held up her mug, and we toasted. "Here's to drowning our sorrows." We downed the beers. "Hold on, I'll be right back." Ellie got up and made her way to the bar. She said something to Marcus and then pointed over to me. Marcus reached under the counter and then set out two shot glasses, a bottle of Jose Cuervo, a salt shaker, and a highball glass filled with lime wedges. He moved it to a tray and then slid it over to Ellie. She carried it back to our table and sat. "It's time to kick this up a notch."

She filled two shot glasses with tequila then handed me a lime.

"Here's to telling people how we really feel at two o'clock in the morning."

"Let's not call anyone at two, okay?"

Ellie giggled. "Deal."

And then we both downed our shots.

She refilled them, and again, we held them up.

"This is for all the phony-ass friends who've come out of the woodwork to tell me that they suspected that Lance was gay all along. Bullshit. That's utter bullshit. If they suspected it, then when they RSVP'd to my wedding, they just should have said maybe next time." She swallowed the shot and then looked at me.

"Yeah, I got nothing for that one." I did another shot.

Ellie fixed two more shots and then held one up in the air. "Here's to my inner bitch, may she stay locked away in her cell tonight." Ellie finished off her third shot.

Before downing mine, I asked, "Are you an angry drunk?"

"No, just a loud one."

I downed my third shot. I could handle loud.

"And I like to stand up for my friends. You're now my friend. Want to toilet paper your ex's house?"

"She isn't really my ex." I settled into the warmth spreading through me and shrugged. "Well, maybe she is my ex, as in ex-friend. Never mind, let's just drink."

And drink we did.

"Oh shit, I love this song. Come on, you have to dance with me." Ellie stood but then quickly grabbed the table.

"Maybe we shouldn't dance."

"No. I want to dance. This is a sate grong. I mean great song. It's Garth Brooks. Like my name, but no relation. Did you hear me?"

"Yes, I heard you."

"We aren't related to Garth. Even though our last name is Brooks. What's your last name?"

"Kinkaide."

"Koolaid?"

"No, Kinkaide."

"Ohhh. Let's dance." Ellie held on to me and belted out the lyrics to "I've Got Friends in Low Places."

I tried to follow the crowd as they moved in some formation to the song, but standing upright took almost all of my concentration. When the song was over, we made our way back to the table and I laid my head down. Ellie shoved another shot at me.

"Drink up," she urged.

Not bothering with the lime or salt, I downed the tequila straight. "I loved her. I fucking loved her, man."

"I'm not a man."

"No. Not you. I know you aren't a man. Me, I'm the man."

"Ohhh."

"But I loved her. I can't believe she'd do this to me, to us. You know? She ruined us. You know what?"

"What?" Ellie leaned in, ready for me to share some big secret.

"I bought a ring. I've always known that Paris was the one for me. Yep, been saving up for a long time. Now she'll never see that damn ring. It sucks." I only lifted my head when I felt a tap on my shoulder.

"Weed. You're here. Asher, this is my little brudder Weed."

Reid shook his head. "What the fuck is up with the baby talk? You're drunk."

"He's drunker." Ellie pointed at me.

I held up my thumb and squinted at the two Marcuses standing next to Reid.

"See?"

"All I see is that both of you are shit-faced. Come on, I'm taking you two home."

I heard my brother's voice, but I couldn't understand what he was saying. "Uhhh?"

"Ash, I'm closing tonight, so I was just going to crash upstairs. You can't go in the house like this, you'll wake Mom. Reid said that you can go to his house and stay in his spare room. Okay?"

I gave another thumbs up. Or, at least, I think I gave a thumbs up.

"Take their phones away from them. I constantly had to keep an eye on the two of them because they were calling god knows who."

"Will do," Reid said to Marcus before turning to the both of us. "Can either of you walk?"

"Sure we can walk. Can't we walk, Ashey?"

Ashey? What the fuck. Whatever. "Uh huh. I can walk." I felt my chair being slid out and then someone helping me stand.

"Here. We'll help each other." Ellie wrapped her arms around me.

"Oh god, this is going to be good," Reid mumbled.

My brother was laughing. "Where's my phone? I need a picture of this."

Stumbling but holding on to Ellie, I felt Reid's hand on my back as he pushed us forward. "My truck is to the left." We headed off toward where several pickups were parked, and Reid corrected us. "Nope, your other left." He chuckled.

My head was spinning as I squinted to try to focus on what was in front of me. But nothing made any sense. Bringing one hand up to my eyes, I made an open fist and tried to peer through it, as if my hand was a telescope, totally hoping that was my best option. Only, it wasn't. As soon as I did it, the earth under my feet pitched and I stumbled. I probably would have eaten it if it weren't for Reid grabbing a fistful of my shirt to keep me upright.

"Okay, you two, over here. That's it. Right here. Okay, just rest against the truck."

My back hit the cool metal right before my legs slowly gave way, and then the small pebbles from the gravel-covered parking lot bit into my skin through my jeans.

"You fell down. Ashey fell down. Did you see that, Weed?" Ellie started laughing.

"Yep, I saw that. Okay, Ell, I'm going to put you in the front."

"Don't leave him. You can't leave him, Weed."

"Calm down, Ellie, I'm not leaving him. I can only handle one of you drunk idiots at a time."

"Oh."

"Yeah, oh."

Reid and his sister kept arguing, and their voices were so fucking loud. The door shut, and my body shook from the vibration. I was confused by the sound of another door opening, and then, once again, Ellie's laughter seemed to fill the air. "Okay, Asher, on the count of three, I'm going to pull you by your arms, but you're going to have to help. Hear me?"

"Yep." I tried to give him a thumbs up, but he had hold of my hands. I was being shoved into a seat and then buckled in.

"God, you two are going to owe me," Reid bitched.

PARIS

"*A*re you coming, Paris?" London hollered.

"Be right there. I'm just grabbing some coffee." I'd been "grabbing coffee" for almost ten minutes. I wasn't trying to piss London off on purpose, but I needed a few minutes to take in everything that had just happened. Cora Kelly was back . . . in our lives. "Anyone else want some? It's decaf."

"No. I want to make this quick, I'm tired."

Filling my mug, I headed into the living room and turned as Holland came in through the front door. She'd walked Cora out to her car.

"Dickhead Brooks must be having a wild party. He just pulled into his driveway, and I can hear some girl laughing. She sounds like a fucking hyena."

"Enough. I want to talk about what all we just learned." London plopped onto the couch. "I don't believe one damn thing she said. I know there isn't a huge age difference between us, but I wasn't sad to see her go all those years ago. You two may not remember, but it was miserable around here. We never knew whether she'd be here when we woke up or not. Dad was a much happier person after she was gone."

"Really? She sounded so sincere." I was shocked that London wasn't caving even a little.

"You're going to tell me that you believe Dad refused to let her see us?"

"Well . . . no. But maybe she took it that way." I couldn't imagine anyone lying over something like this or why. What did she have to gain by coming now?

"You're being delusional, Paris. She's after something. She's always had an ulterior motive. She's probably after more money."

"More money? What are you talking about?" I leaned forward and braced my elbows on my knees.

"After Dad died, I was reconciling the home accounts and found several canceled checks that Dad had sent her. It wasn't much, but it wasn't anything to scoff at either."

"How much are we talking?"

"A thousand here, five thousand there, but over the years, it had equaled almost fifty thousand dollars."

"Fuck." Holland's word came out in a whoosh of breath.

"Tell me about it. I discovered it when we were strapped and having to do our own tightening down all because of the fire. What I wouldn't have given to have had that fifty grand back." London reached for my mug, and I let her have it. She rolled it between her palms, as if letting the heat from the mug infuse her with some silent energy before she took a long sip.

"So, you think she's here for money?" I asked even though I didn't believe it. It sounded so cold, so calculating. And all I could hear was Daddy saying that I was like my mom. I couldn't imagine ever doing something like that.

"I do. Why else would she come back after all this time?"

"I have no idea." I took my mug back from her and turned to Holland, who was rubbing her temples as if to combat a headache.

"Whatever she's here for, we are not giving it to her. Right now, all I want to do is sleep."

"Me too." London stood and then grabbed Holland's hand to help her up.

"Night, you two." I curled my legs up under me.

They both mumbled as they shuffled away, and when they were gone, I grabbed the afghan off the back of the couch and pulled it over me.

Mom, my mom, was back just when I needed her most. Asher was gone and never coming back. How had my life turned so pear-shaped in a week? Closing my eyes, I felt the tears start to fall. I hadn't cried as much in my entire life as I had lately. I was feeling so betrayed by everyone—Asher for changing our relationship, Wally for telling my mom about our family, myself for not knowing my own mind. I cried for betraying my sisters. I knew that London wanted Cora gone, but I wanted her here.

I couldn't take all of this anymore. If anyone asked me what was wrong, I'd tell them that I'd gone crazy. That I'd checked out somewhere between the snake rattling and locking me in that damn freezer and Cora returning and making me feel like I was seven years old all over again.

"Paris. Paris, wake up."

I jerked up and groaned. "Ugh. What time is it?" I stretched and heard my neck pop. Rolling my shoulders, I tried to work out the kinks from sleeping funny.

"It's just after five. Here's the baby monitor. Braden's at our house getting ready to leave for work. I'm going to go check on the cattle. I'll be back." London tossed me the small speaker before she headed for the front door.

I stood and stretched before refolding the blanket and draping it over the couch before heading to my bedroom to change and then start my day.

Sitting on the side of the bed, I pulled on my cowboy boots then walked over to my dresser. I usually hated sleeping in earrings, but then again, I usually didn't sleep on the couch either, so I switched my small silver hoops out for some turquoise butterflies and then headed to the kitchen.

Living in an area that most people had never heard of on the outskirts of Orlando, Florida, made it almost impossible to find people to help on the ranch. It was why my sisters and I were always at Daddy's side while we were growing up. Not that we minded one bit. London loved helping Dad corral the cattle, and Holland could spend her entire life in the saddle. She was a natural equestrian and full of energy, which made her a great riding instructor. But me? I wanted to be inside cooking. I wanted to be the reason they all came home and sat around the table.

I pulled out the canister of grits from the pantry and a rasher of bacon from the fridge, wishing I hadn't spent the night on the couch. I had a crick in my neck, and my shoulder felt stiff, but it was more annoying than painful as I gathered everything to make breakfast. Holland walked in as I was pulling a pot out of the cabinet, and I gave her a smile over my shoulder.

"Morning." She was busy texting. "Breakfast will be ready in a few."

"Mm-hmm."

The front door opened and shut, and London headed

straight back to the bathroom before crossing the hallway to Tera's room.

"I haven't heard a peep through the monitor. She still asleep?" I asked when London entered the kitchen, looking a bit pensive.

"Yeah, she is a great sleeper, a sure sign that our next will be colicky."

Oh shit, was she trying to find a way to tell us something? Hell, they weren't even supposed to be having sex yet. "Are you already talking about a second baby?" I was shocked that my sister, who'd never wanted to be a mom, was so eager to be a mother of two.

"Yeah, we don't want to wait too long. I love having you two as sisters, but it would have been more fun had we all been closer in age."

I nodded, totally agreeing with London, then turned back to removing the bacon from the grease. We were each three years apart, so we didn't fight about typical girl stuff, like borrowing each other's clothes, since we were never close to the same sizes while in school, and we never fought over boys, since we weren't usually in the same schools. But we did fight over sister stuff, like being in each other's space, or who got to watch what on television. Once, Dad had threatened to tape Holland and London together if they didn't stop arguing over who was looking at whom for too long.

Truthfully, though, it would have been nice to double date, go to football games, or hang out with my sisters at school. At least I thought it would have been. I'd probably feel totally different if we'd have been close in age.

"Did you tell her?" London whispered to Holland while I was trying to consider age gaps in siblings.

"Tell me what?" I handed a giant plate of bacon to London to take to the table, then filled three bowls with grits.

I let out a sigh as I stared at the simplicity of the grits and bacon. Just over a week ago this never would have been our breakfast, it never would have been so simple. Once upon a time, not so long ago, like less than a month, we had a house full, with Asher and Marcus and usually Braden with us.

Tuning in to London and Holland, who were still whispering, I asked, "Tell me what?" I took my seat then dropped a dollop of butter into my bowl of grits and started crumbling some bacon on top of it.

"Paris, you really don't feel anything for Asher?" Holland asked.

"He's my best friend—or rather, he was. Of course I feel something for him. But he was willing to sacrifice almost thirty years of friendship all because of some misguided notion that he loves me."

"Are you absolutely, positively sure you don't feel anything for him, as in, being in love with him?" London's eyes bore into me as if she were searching for some unannounced truth. But I wasn't lying. I truly loved him, but as my best friend.

"I want more. I want to be wooed. I want love notes and flowers and poetry. I don't think romance is too much to ask for, do you?"

"No. But have you ever really given him a chance? You two could take things slow?"

"Slow? They've taken twenty-nine years," Holland added.

"What sort of boundaries? Asher wants more than I do. And how well would that work out if I realized before him that we were on a path of destruction, but he thought we were bound for happily ever after? No." I shook my head, resigning myself to my decision. "I'm not in love with him. Anything that I do will be unfair to Asher. I'm not sure how many times I have to explain that to everyone."

London shook her head, obviously disappointed in my answer.

"Well, then you're not going to care that Asher left the bar with some blonde last night."

Wow, it was as if she'd just exploded a bomb in the middle of my chest. I was mourning the loss of our friendship, and he was dicking around. "I wouldn't care. I would feel vindicated. He claimed to have been in love with me since we were in middle school, and he is already picking up another woman? It just proves I was right." Yeah, that was what it proved. "How do you know he took someone home last night?"

"Remember Cassie? She graduated a year before me. She sent me a text. For some reason, she thought you and Asher had gotten married, so when she saw him leave with someone who wasn't you, she was worried and thought someone in the family should know."

Fuck. It was hard to breathe. "I'm not feeling so well. Maybe I'm coming down with a cold from being in that freezer for so long. I'm going to go lie down." My excuse was weak, but it was all I could think of. I just needed to get away from everyone at that moment.

"Wait." London grabbed my hand, and I turned and met two sets of chocolate-brown eyes. They were identical to mine. "Do you want to talk about this?"

"What's there to talk about? I'm fine. I just don't feel well. And Asher can sleep with whomever he wants." I pushed back my chair but froze when my eyes caught sight of a car pulling in front of the house. "Who drives a Ford Focus?"

"That's Mom's rental car." Holland stood to confirm her answer.

"I'm leaving." London pushed back her chair.

"No. You need to be here. We need to get through this and figure out what we're going to do." I tried to stay calm, torn between wanting to lay down and just sleep and wanting to piece my family back together. I was losing everyone . . . my daddy, Asher . . . I couldn't lose anyone else. We needed to stay together.

"What do you mean, what we're going to do? The woman suddenly reappears after more than twenty years and blames it all on Dad, how convenient. I'm sorry, but if Braden turned out to be an ass, you better believe I'd have his ass in court and would have Tera with me. I would never leave my daughter behind. And I definitely would not be accepting checks from him. We don't need her in our lives. Don't tell me you want her around." London peered at me, waiting for an answer.

"Well . . ." I looked out the window and watched her climb out of her car. I was fidgeting, and I knew it. "I'd like to see if there's any truth in what she's saying. We all view things differently." The doorbell rang, but no one moved to answer it.

"I don't care one way or the other. I don't remember her, and I don't want to know her, so she can stay or go, makes no difference to me." Holland returned to eating.

"Fine, I'll answer the door." I headed off. Rolling back my shoulders, I inhaled deeply, the smell of fresh-cooked bacon still heavy in the air.

"I'm getting Tera, and we're going to my house. I'll use the back door." London headed off.

I twisted the large brass knob and stepped back as I opened the door. "Hi, Cora . . . Mom. Come in." She reached up and placed a quick kiss on my cheek.

"Hi, darling. I missed you." She walked in and glanced over at the kitchen. "Hello, Holland."

"Hmm." Holland gave her a mock salute and kept eating.

"London isn't here? I thought I saw her through the window."

"She went out the back, she needed to get home."

"Oh. Sorry I missed her."

I didn't want to say anything, but that was the understatement of the year. "So, what brings you by?"

"Can't a mom just come over and see her girls?" She headed toward the kitchen table and dropped her purse onto the counter.

"Yeah. I guess so. This is all just so new to me, and it's a lot to get used to. But we will learn, no worries."

Cora made herself comfortable at the table while Paris grabbed her a plate and dished out some food. Cora started eating before Paris had even sat back down. Holland looked like she wanted to say something, and I just watched in uncomfortable silence. We allowed everyone over, people never knocked on the door, why not her too?

Holland stopped eating. "Can I ask you something?"

"Sure, anything." Cora sounded as if she hadn't a care in the world.

"Where have you been? What have you been doing since you left us when I was three?"

"When I first left, I took a bus to Nashville. I waited tables and met some country singers. Nashville is beautiful, everyone has a dream of making it big and signing. A lot of the restaurants and bars had open-mic nights, and talent scouts would come in and just sit and listen. I always wondered if I was waiting on the next Randy Travis. But I always thought about you three girls." Cora put her fork down long enough to pat my hand, as if to emphasize her point. "From there, I headed out west. I stopped in Vegas and was a card dealer for a while. Did you know that men will toss you coins worth five and ten thousand dollars just for a lucky kiss? But it wasn't for me. I wanted to be an actress, so after that, I spent some time in Los Angeles. But I wasn't one to be tied down, so I didn't stay there long. But you three

77

girls were never far from my mind. I always wondered what you were up to."

I looked at Holland, and she rolled her eyes. Clearly, she didn't believe Cora, but I *wanted* to believe her. What mother wouldn't be thinking about her children?

ASHER

*D*id we at least shoot the horse that kicked me upside the head? 'Cause, seriously, I felt like my head was going to explode. "Fuuuccckkk."

"Ah, you're awake."

I focused on trying to open one eye just a crack, but my eyes felt crusty. "Marcus?"

"Do I sound like Marcus?"

I racked my brain for what in the fuck Marcus sounded like, and after I managed to clear away the haze, I finally realized that, no, it didn't sound like Marcus. "No?"

"Of course no, you idiot. Do you not remember anything from last night?"

I thought back.

Bar. Drinking. Blonde girl. Tequila.

"Ellie?"

"Do I sound like a fucking Ellie?"

"No?"

"Would you just open your damn eyes? It's me, Reid. I'm Ellie's brother. I brought both of your drunk asses home last night. Fuck. You two were exhausting. Anyway, here's some water and aspirin. Drink up."

I reached out, patting for the bottle.

"Open your damn eyes."

"It hurts."

"Yep, and you two deserve it. Fucking idiots. Breakfast is ready, or should I say lunch?"

"Lunch?"

"You really are a man of few words, aren't you? Yeah, lunch. It's almost noon. I hope you weren't working today because, if you were, you're late. I tried to wake you earlier, but I gave up after about thirty minutes."

I leaned up and rested on one elbow and took the aspirin and water from him. "Thanks, Reid. I'm sorry."

"Yeah, I'll add it to my bill. I'm going to go try to wake the she-beast. Why don't you get yourself up, and I'll meet you in the kitchen." I tried to give him the peace sign, but I wasn't sure whether it was with one finger or two. And the way my luck was running, it was probably the wrong one sticking up. The last thing I needed to do was piss off the guy who rescued me.

I swallowed the aspirin and downed the bottle of water, wishing I could sleep for the rest of the day but knowing it was no use. After I was sure I wasn't going to vomit, I hauled my hungover ass out of the bed I was in.

I looked like hell, but at least there was a brand-new toothbrush and tube of toothpaste waiting for me in the bathroom. I patted my hair down the best I could, then brushed my teeth twice to get rid of the grime coating them, and the rank taste in my mouth. I swore I could smell the Elbow Room leaking out my pores, and it sure as hell was imbedded in my clothes.

After giving myself a quick look over in the mirror and finally deciding this was the best I was going to get, I followed the noise to the kitchen. Reid and Ellie were sitting at the table. Ellie, who looked like I felt, was wearing sunglasses inside and clutching a mug to her chest.

"You two look like shit. Here, you can have these back now." Reid set my phone and what I assumed was Ellie's phone onto the table. "Next time you two decide to get drunk, leave your phones at home."

Ellie let out a giggle.

"Ah, god no."

"God yes. Look at your call logs; they are extensive. You're going to have some serious explaining to do today."

I scrolled through the dialed numbers: Paris . . . fifteen seconds, Paris, Paris for twenty minutes. Paris, Paris. "Holy shit. I called Paris five times."

Ellie was still giggling.

"What's so fucking funny?" I glared at her.

"I think it was my fault."

"How was it your fault?"

"I think I convinced you to call her. We played Cyrano de Bergerac, and I was your wingman. I fed you all the lines to say."

"We played what?"

"Cyrano. You know, he's the one with all the words, so he hides in the bushes and feeds others the lines of what to say for him?"

"I know who Cyrano de Bergerac is, I just never imagined playing it. Please tell me that you remember what we said?" Because I had a voicemail from the ranch's house number, and I was pretty sure I didn't want to look at it.

Ellie wrinkled her nose and thought for a second. "No. I just remember you were shitty at repeating what I told you to say."

Great. Ellie could have had me say anything. For all I knew, I cussed Paris out, or worse, made an even bigger ass of myself and drove a bigger wedge between us and confessed my love for her . . . again. I groaned and, knowing I couldn't ignore it, I hit the transcript icon and read the message.

ASHER, *it's Holland. Maleficent is looking distended. I think the insemination worked this time. When you get a chance, can you swing by? Need to know if I should increase her vitamins.*

THAT WAS SO MUCH BETTER than what I had expected to see, so I pulled up my texts.

ME: I'll swing by today and check her out for you. It will be later, though, is that okay?

Holland: Thanks. Give me a heads up when you're on your way and I'll meet you at the stables.

Me: Will do.

Holland: Not to be nosey, but are you okay? I got a text this morning about you and a certain blonde.

Me: Oh god, don't ask.

Holland: Believe me, I won't. Just surprised.

Me: Not more than me.

Holland: Doubt that. Way to keep up your reputation, Doc.

WHY THE HELL was Holland so angry? This had to be about more than just me getting drunk. Hell, it wasn't that long ago I was driving her home from her own night of overindulgence. I turned and looked at Ellie, then shook my head. It couldn't be. There was no way that Holland would think that me and Ellie...she knew me better than that. Fuck, she was fully aware that I was in love with her sister.

"Everything okay?" Ellie asked, clearly concerned that her little game had made things worse for me. "Paris pissed?"

"Everything's fine. It was for work. It was her younger sister—"

Reid let out a groan.

"She asked if I could swing by and check on a horse. I guess I'll find out how pissed Paris is when I get there."

"Can I go with you? Please? I need to get out of here, and if I'm going to volunteer with you, then I might as well start now, right?"

I thought about what Ellie had asked and seriously doubted this being such a good idea but then halted. Maybe it was exactly what Holland, and more importantly, Paris, needed. If they had heard about Ellie, then they needed to meet Ellie and see that there was nothing between us.

"What?" Reid interrupted.

"Asher and I talked about this yesterday. I'm going to volunteer as his vet tech."

Reid arched a brow. "And you two obviously made great decisions last night."

I smiled at Reid's candor. He sounded like London or Marcus when they were talking to Paris and me when we were younger. "We talked about it before we got drunk, thank you very much. I've been dying to do something. Besides, it isn't as if I need the money."

"I'm going to run home and get changed." I slid my phone to Ellie. "Here, put in your number, and I'll text you when I'm ready. I can swing by and get you." I waited for her to enter her number and hand me my phone back. "Thanks for everything, Reid, I really appreciate it."

"Anytime. You need a ride to go get your truck?"

"Nah, my brother should be home. I'll have him take me.

83

You've done enough. If I can do anything to repay you, don't hesitate to ask."

"Go. You rescued me the other night with Holland. I consider us even. By the way, how do you put up with her?"

* * *

I WASN'T AS FAST as I had hoped, and it was almost four o'clock by the time I picked up Ellie and we were pulling down the drive and around the side to the Iron Horse Stables. Ellie let out a low whistle when she saw it. "Impressive."

"It's like a fairytale. At least that's what Paris says. If you only knew the number of times she made me pretend to be Prince Charming and rescue her, whether she was Snow White, Sleeping Beauty, or some other princess I can't think of." Paris was thirteen when her dad decided to build the new stable and replace the old barn. Thinking back, it probably wasn't the best idea to have a ten, thirteen, and sixteen-year-old offering input. It was the one area that had stood out in stark contrast to the rest of the farm with archways, wain-scot walls, and a gabled roof.

"Did she have to twist your arm to get you to play along?" Ellie winked.

"Shut up."

"So, tell me about their stables."

"Well, the stables started out as a hobby for them, but Holland—she's the youngest of the three sisters—runs them. She teaches Western riding."

"Holland, as in the bane of my brother's existence, right?"

"Yep, one and the same. Anyway, they usually have ten to twelve quarter horses at any given time. Oh, just a heads up, the horses all have strange names. Maybe not so strange when you think about the whole fairytale aspect. But it is sort of funny. London, she's the oldest—"

"Wait. London? So, there's London, Holland, and Paris?"

"Yeah." I let out a short laugh. "Their mom wanted to see the world, so she gave the girls names of foreign places. London is married, and she and her husband just had their first baby. She is totally opposite. She likes being right here, so she named her daughter Tera."

"I don't get it."

"As in Terra . . . meaning earth."

"Gee, Reid and I just got good old family names."

"Ellie is a family name?"

"My real name is Ellis, and yes, it's my mom's maiden name. Reid was her mom's maiden name. So, finish telling me about the horses' names."

"Oh, they're named after Disney villains. Today, we're seeing Maleficent. But there's also Tremaine—"

"Okay, I know Maleficent, she's from *Sleeping Beauty*, but I've never heard of Tremaine."

"She's the evil stepmother from *Cinderella*. That's Paris's horse." I pulled in front of the stables and parked. Grabbing my medical bag, I got out, Ellie following behind just as Holland walked out.

"Hey, Ash—"

"Holland, sorry I had to push you back. Had a crazy night." Ellie punched me in the side. "What?"

"Don't say that, it sounded bad," she whispered to me.

What sounded bad? I said the truth. "Anyway, this is Ellie. She's a vet tech and is familiar with large animals. She's going to start helping me."

"Oh. Well, then . . . nice to meet you, Ellie."

I gave Holland a weird look, because she wasn't smiling and wasn't offering to shake Ellie's hand, even though Ellie held hers out.

"Nice to meet you, Holland. You have a beautiful stable. Asher was telling me that you teach Western. I'd love to learn."

"You don't ride?" Holland gave me a quizzical look.

"No. I mean, yes. Yes, I do ride, just not Western. I ride English."

"Growing up around here, there wasn't too much need for English." Holland turned around and walked off, totally dismissing Ellie.

"I'm sorry, Ellie." I held up my hands.

"Don't be. She's choosing sides, and she has just let it be known that she is on her sister's."

"Her sister's? For what?"

"Men. You all are so stupid sometimes. Holland obviously thinks you and Paris belong together, and that I'm here to destroy that."

"Let me go explain. I'm sorry, I should have been more clear."

"Don't you dare. A little competition is good every now and then."

"You don't get it, Paris isn't the jealous sort."

"We'll see." Ellie patted my arm and followed Holland into the stables.

"This is Maleficent." I rubbed the muzzle of a black mare. "You're right, she does look a little distended."

"Ahh, are we having a baby?" Ellie clapped her hands. "Who's the papa?"

"The Good Humor man," Holland replied.

"Holland." I snapped. "It was—"

Ellie held up a hand. "I got it, Ash, frozen semen. Pretty common for horses . . . so was the punchline."

I shook my head, not wanting to be in the middle of a catfight. Slipping on an OB sleeve, I slathered my hand and the lower part of my arm with OB grease and walked to the side of the horse. Holland had already restrained her. This was the nice part of working with knowledgeable animal owners.

People always thought my job as a veterinarian sounded fun, but this definitely wasn't the glamorous part of my job.

"Okay, Maleficent, this isn't going to feel great, and I'm sorry for that." I moved forward with the examination, feeling along the reproductive tract for small palpitations and trying to find either the amniotic sac or feel a change in the uterus.

"Aha, there we are." Pulling my hand out, I slipped off my glove and dropped it into the garbage before heading to the small utility sink in the corner. "You were right, she's pregnant. Let's cut out the fescue and just give her other feed. You know the rest."

Horses were pregnant for almost a year, tall fescue, a type of grass, increased their gestation period. Even though I was a man, that still sounded horrid. And that was one of the least problematic side effects.

"I do. Thanks, Ash, I'll start increasing nutrients in January." Holland walked over to a giant calendar she had pinned to the wall and counted out seven months from today.

"We're going to get out of here, then. See you." I dropped my supplies back into my bag. Ellie was finger combing Maleficent's mane.

"I was hoping you were going to go up to the house. We've had some crazy changes. But you have too, obviously." Holland shot daggers over toward Ellie.

"Stop." I tried to think of how to say this without sounding heartless, because I definitely wasn't that. I just didn't want to be hurt anymore. "I need time."

"Will you excuse us for a second, Emily?"

"Ellie, her name is Ellie, and she's fine. She knows all about Paris."

"Really, Asher?"

"Holland, if you'd stop being a brat—"

"How dare you. Now you sound like Dick Brooks next door."

Ellie busted out laughing. "Dick Brooks. Oh my god, that is great."

Holland snarled at Ellie.

"Stop, Holland. Your sister has made it clear that she wants someone else. I don't know who, and truthfully, I don't want to know. But as far as being mean to Ellie, there is no reason. And for your information, Reid is Ellie's brother."

Ellie gave a small wave. "Yep, that's me."

"Two reasons not to like you now," Holland mumbled under her breath.

"I'm out of here. I'm sorry that you've all had changes, but they don't include me. Call me when you need me as a veterinarian." With that, I strode out the wide-open stable door, but stopped when I saw London coming from the house. As she got closer, I realized it wasn't London. It was an older version of her. Holy shit. "Cora?"

"Yes. I'm sorry, do I know you?"

"You do—or rather, did. I'm Asher Kinkaide. I live next door. I'm the vet."

"Asher? Oh my, look at you. You're all grown and handsome. I guess your father retired."

"My father passed away a couple of years ago."

"I'm sorry to hear that. And who is this?" Cora turned her focus on Ellie.

"Hi, I'm Ellie. I'm Asher's vet assistant. It's very nice to meet you, Cora."

Holland came out of the stables, closing the doors behind

her. When she turned, she wasn't looking at us. I followed her line of sight and instantly regretted it.

Paris was walking toward us.

She was wearing cutoffs, cowboy boots, and some ruffle-type shirt she always wore. She was beautiful. When our eyes locked, she stopped and gave me a small smile. But her smile fell when she looked beyond me and saw Ellie.

I never should have agreed to let Ellie tag along.

"Paris, do you remember when you were little and you and Asher used to be inseparable?" Cora asked.

"Yes, I remember. We were inseparable until about ten days ago." She sounded hurt, and that was the last thing I'd wanted. God, I had loved the woman, I *still* loved her, but she'd destroyed me.

It's amazing how things don't turn out the way we plan, isn't it?

"Yes, it is," Cora answered, because apparently, I'd said the last part aloud. "Nothing is ever the way we intended."

Paris's attention was fixed on Ellie, and being the lady she was, she made the first move. "Hi, I'm Paris."

"I'm Ellie. I'm just here helping Asher."

"That's nice of you. I've never met you. How do you know each other?"

"She's Reid's sister," I said at the same time Ellie replied, "We got drunk together last night."

"You got drunk?" Paris asked. I could feel the weight of her eyes as she tried to see through me and find the truth.

"Long story." I waved it off.

"And night," Ellie replied with a laugh.

"Can you keep quiet?" Holland barked to Ellie. "Now I totally see the family resemblance."

"I better go." I took a step toward my truck. "Cora, you look great." I couldn't say it was nice seeing her, because it wasn't. I'd heard too much about the woman to believe she was anything other than bad news. "Holland, holler if you need anything. Paris, you're beautiful as always." I took a few more steps and paused right by Paris, trying to decide if I should say anything else. "I miss you."

"Obviously not," she whispered.

"Why would you say that?" Paris swerved her eyes toward Ellie. "You have no clue what you're talking about." I strode to my truck and jumped in, Ellie close on my heels.

"She loves you, you know that, right?" Ellie said softly as I backed out of the driveway.

"Yeah, as a friend."

"No, she loves you as more than that."

"I think you misread the situation. Besides, if Cora is back, things are only going to get worse."

PARIS

J waited until the truck was out of sight. "I'm not feeling so well. I'm going to go lie down. Dinner's ready, just help yourselves."

"Paris, wait."

"Not now, Holland."

"Paris." My sister grabbed my hand, but I yanked loose.

"Want me to come with you?" Cora asked.

"No. I just want to be alone, truly. I don't feel well."

I'd been walking the short distance between the stables and our house for most of my life, but never had the journey seemed so long. Every root that had broken through the ground seemed to be reaching up with the sole purpose of making me stumble. It was almost as if every jagged rock was on a mission to roll in my way and trip me. And damn it all to hell, where did all these friggin' tiny pebbles come from? For some reason, they all seemed to be bouncing into my boots as I ran as fast as I could toward the front porch. I took the stairs two at a time, shoved through the front door, and hightailed it down the hallway to my room, slamming my door shut and twisting the lock behind me. Slowly, I slid down until my butt rested on the hardwood, pulled up my legs, and dropped my head against my knees.

What was happening to me? Why did I feel this way? I didn't care that Asher got drunk and took someone home? I mean . . . it wasn't as if he hadn't dated, hadn't gotten drunk with other women, right? It shouldn't bother me.

I thought long and hard for a moment.

Who was I kidding?

Yes, yes, I did care. The truth was, I couldn't think of one woman Asher had ever dated. Sure, he had to have gone out in college, but if he did, he didn't tell me about it. He was almost thirty, for crying out loud, it wasn't as if he was a virgin. The man was attractive and smart. Women probably threw themselves at him.

But if what he claimed were true, if he'd truly loved me, how could he move on so fast? He'd hurt me. Yeah, that was it. What I was feeling—it was hurt. I was hurt because he lied to me. He lied about loving me when he didn't. Love wasn't over in ten days. It wasn't that cut and dried.

My body bounced as Holland and London knocked on the door. "Paris, let us in. We want to talk to you."

"I don't feel well."

"Open the door. You and I both know that isn't the problem." London's voice was soft.

"Oh, really? How do you know?"

"I know because I saw your face when you saw Ellie here with him. You're in love with him, but you're either too blind to see it, or too dumb to admit it. Open up. Let's talk."

"Can you give me a few minutes? I'll be out there." I slowly pulled myself up.

"I'll set the table," Holland said, walking off.

"Will you let me in? Please?" I dropped my chin and took a deep breath. She wasn't going to let this go. I twisted the lock and let her in.

"Where's Tera?"

"She's taking a nap."

"Where's Mom?"

"Cora's in the living room." London refused to call her anything but Cora, claiming that no true mother would ever leave. "I want to ask you something, and I want you to really think hard on it."

"Okay, what?"

"How did you feel when you saw that woman with Asher today? Be honest."

"I thought she was rude. She kept saying things under her breath to him."

"I didn't ask what you thought of her. I asked how you felt."

"I didn't think she was his type."

London quirked a brow. "You're evading my question."

I buried my face in my hands. "Betrayed." The answer was instant, and I hated that I'd said it.

"Why?"

"Because he lied to me. He claimed to have been in love with me, yet he's already with another woman. That isn't love. At least not any type of love that I know or want."

"You're making excuses."

"No, I'm not." I glared at her, totally defending my stance.

"So, you're telling me that, had Asher not claimed his love for you, you'd have been okay if he showed up here with a beautiful woman and wanted us to meet her?"

"She's working for him."

"You can't have it both ways. Either you feel betrayed that he's with a pretty woman, or you're dismissing her because she works for him." London raised her brow again in challenge.

"Who said she's pretty? I didn't think she was all that pretty. She was kind of gangly, to be honest."

DANIELLE NORMAN

The corner of London's mouth raised into a smirk.

"What? I'm just being honest."

"Spoken like a truly jealous woman. Well, you think about what I asked you. Really think about it because, if you discover that you're in love with him like I think you are, then you better get your ass in gear, or you're gonna lose him forever. Asher isn't the kind of man who keeps coming back, only to get rejected." London strolled out of my room, leaving me to follow.

I didn't know how I felt about him. But London wasn't wrong. I needed to figure it out because Asher, although never the dominant, alpha type, was definitely the alpha-beta. He was the kind of man who would open the door for me during the day and throw me against it at night. He wasn't the type of man to walk over me, but he wouldn't allow me to walk over him either. And somehow he found time to take care of everything. I knew once I made my decision, I better be one hundred percent positive because regardless, Asher wasn't the type to try again. He had way too much pride.

Feeling a sense of resolve wash over me, I joined my family. Sitting at the table with our mom was awkward, so I opted for small talk, even though I didn't want to be there.

"Will Braden be here?" I asked as I passed the basket of fried chicken.

"No, he's running late. There was an accident," London said as she passed the basket on to Cora.

"So, you and Asher are still friends, or should I say were? What happened?" Cora looked curious.

"He told Paris that he loved her, and she shot him down," Holland explained as she took the basket. "Craziest thing she's ever done." Holland wound her index finger next to her temple. Yeah, I got it, she thought I was nuts.

"No. I don't think so. I think Paris made a smart decision. Friends shouldn't be lovers."

"Who asked you?" London's voice was low and curt. "You aren't exactly the poster child for relationships or motherhood."

"Say what you want, London, but some things are learned through experience. I learned that the hard way. Your father and I had been friends long before we got married, and it ruined our friendship and then ruined our marriage."

"But I can't imagine being with anyone else. What would you have me do? Marry someone I didn't love for what? Money? Or just so I can say that we weren't friends?"

"Fine, you'll lose him, and you'll only have yourself to blame. Just because I divorced your father, doesn't mean I didn't love him; I did. But I wanted to go back to being friends, and he wanted marriage or nothing."

Her words were like a punch right into the solar plexus. "That's Asher. He told me that he loves me, and when I told him friendships don't make for good marriages, he gave up on everything. He hasn't talked to me since. Today was the first I'd seen him since, and we used to see each other every day."

"That's how it is." Cora waved her hand toward the heavens, as if preaching. "It's probably not too late to get him back as a friend, but you never will if you try for more. Heed my warning."

"Will you stop?" London threw her fork down. "She'll have nothing if she can't stand to be around him because the guy has moved on. He isn't going to wait around for the rest of his life. Eventually, he will get the hint that Paris doesn't love him, or at least that she is pretending not to, and he'll move on. But it won't be far enough to ease Paris's breaking heart. Because he'll always be our neighbor and our vet. Not to mention a family friend. That means Paris will be forced to see him moving on with another woman. Marrying another woman. Being a father to someone else's kids."

"Stop." I jumped from my seat. "Just stop, will you?"

"No, I won't. I'm tired of you tucking your head in the sand. You're not a fucking ostrich. You need to wake up and see what's in front of you. Damn it, Paris. Why are you doing this to him? Hell, why are you doing this to yourself? Admit it, damn it, just admit it already." London glared at me.

"I love him. I love him so much, it is killing me, but I'm afraid. What if it doesn't work out? What if I lose everything?"

London let out a long breath, her eyes filled with a warmth I hadn't seen in a while. "You've already lost everything. Without him, you are not the sister I know, you're different. Without him, Holland and I have lost you. We are all just waiting on you to see it."

I planted my head into my hands, suddenly not hungry. I couldn't stand the thought of him being with another woman. I was the only one to blame, all of this . . . this . . . whatever the hell I was feeling inside was all my fault. I'd caused it. The hurt Asher was feeling, that was mine too. In fact, while I was thinking about it, Asher was mine as well.

I dropped my hands and looked to London. "What do you suggest?"

"I suggest you think of something to rock his world."

"Like what?" When London offered no answers, I turned my attention to Holland. "You have any ideas?"

"I'd start with sending him a message and asking him to talk." Holland was always so direct.

"Do something romantic," London suggested. "You know how Braden took me on a picnic? You could do something like that. We have the buckboard Daddy used to pull us in for hayrides. Why not plan something romantic and use that?"

"How about if you invite him over here and I go to

London's for the night? You can cook a nice meal and then have the house all to yourselves?" Holland offered. "That is, if London doesn't mind."

"Of course I don't, and I think that is a great idea. Where's your phone? You should call him right now."

I got up and raced to get my phone, which was flashing with notifications of missed calls and waiting voicemails, all of which were from Asher.

Well, shit.

I bit my lip as I pulled up the voicemails. The first voice-mail was muffled and less than fifteen seconds, the second was under five seconds, so I skipped that one and went to the third, which was by far the longest.

"Paris, I love you. How could you do this to me?"

Then I heard a woman, who I assumed was Ellie, say something in the background. It was kind of hard to hear because there was a lot of background noise. It sounded as if they were at the bar. "Tell her you miss her. Oh, and tell her that you want to fuck her."

"Yeah, I want to fuck you, but I can't tell you that. I can only think about that alone."

"Alone? You mast . . . you mast . . . fuck . . . you jerk off thinking about her?"

"All the time. She's so beautiful. God, she's so fucking sexy."

"That's hot. You should tell her that."

"No. I don't want her to know."

I cracked up laughing as I listened to Asher and Ellie go back and forth.

"Kitten . . ."

"Kitten? You call her kitten? Why do you call her kitten? That's cute . . ." Ellie was off on some diatribe about kittens and must have moved away from the phone, because I couldn't make out what she was saying.

"For Halloween one year, I dressed up as Batman, and she teased me." Somewhere in the middle of the explanation, he forgot he was talking to Ellie and started talking to me again. "Do you remember that, Paris? You said I couldn't be Batman because I wasn't a man. I had to be Batboy or Robin." I nodded as I listened, totally remembering. "Then you felt bad because it hurt my feelings, so you dressed up as Catwoman." I placed my fingertips against my lips to stifle the smirk. "But I was still mad at you, so I said you couldn't be Catwoman, you had to be a kitten." I nodded. That was it, I was eight years old again, being called kitten. A name that he continued calling me until ten days ago.

By the time the voicemail was finally over, I was more confident than ever that Asher and I would make a great couple.

God, I wanted to hear his voice, but I needed to do it after Cora left. How rude would it be if I asked her to leave? No, I couldn't do that. The woman had just reconnected with us, right?

I couldn't hide the smile as I walked into the kitchen and put the phone on speaker. I replayed the message for everyone to hear.

London was cracking up laughing. "You need to call that man and put him out of his misery."

"And give his right hand a break," Holland said between laughs.

"That's so rude, and the fact that he'd talk about you like that in front of another woman shows he has no respect for you." Cora shook her head in disgust.

"It shows no such thing. It proves there is nothing between Ellie and Asher. It shows that, even when the man is drunk and out of his mind, he's still thinking about Paris," London defended.

"Who wants a man who gets drunk like that anyway?"

"Obviously not you, but then again, you didn't want a hardworking, sober one either." London pushed back her chair. "I'm getting Tera and going home. Sorry, I've had enough 'motherly' advice for one evening."

Cora reached for her, but London pulled back. "Don't go. I really wish you'd stay. I want to get to know you."

"You want something, but that isn't it. I just haven't figured out what it is . . . yet. But I will." London grabbed the baby monitor and headed down the hallway to get Tera, who she still had not allowed Cora to see.

We sat at the table and ate in silence. I was busy thinking of all the possibilities. My mom was sitting opposite me, staring at me and silently telling me not to do what I was about to do. I could feel it. She was giving off some silent vibe. When we were finally done eating, I quickly cleared away the dishes, hoping it would encourage Cora to get on her way as well. Yeah, luck was not on my side tonight.

"Let's have some coffee. I have so many questions to ask you girls. It's why I was hoping that London would finally stay."

I fought the urge to groan and met Holland's eyes. She just shrugged, then got up and helped me clean up the table. Ten minutes later, we were drinking coffee and eating my most recent batch of oatmeal chocolate chip cookies.

"Tell me about you girls. Boyfriends?" Cora took a bite and smiled at us.

"None for me, but obviously Asher for Paris," Holland pointed out.

Cora let out a sigh. She was trying too hard to make up for lost time and had no clue how. "What can I do for you girls? Tell me, what do you feel like you missed out on while I wasn't around?"

"You mean like everything having a mother includes?" Holland asked, shoving an entire cookie into her mouth to stop herself from talking. At least she knew that baiting the woman would not help my cause of getting her to leave early so I could call Asher.

"I always wished that I knew some of your family recipes. Dad said you had been a great cook."

Cora smiled. "Your dad would eat anything, he wasn't picky. But I can write down a few things my grandmother taught me. She used to make the best icebox cake. I'll teach you how to make it."

"Icebox? As in freezer?"

"Nah, icebox is what she called the refrigerator. It was a cold cake, but it was so good. We can make that tomorrow if you want."

"I'd like that." I hated that I was being rude, but I couldn't stop myself from constantly looking over toward the cuckoo clock and checking the time.

This was great and all, and truthfully, I did want to know about her recipes, but I was afraid that by the time she left, it would be too late to call him and he'd be half-asleep. Glancing over at the clock once more, my mom must have caught on to my antsy behavior because let's face it, I was bouncing in my seat.

Mom placed one hand on top of mine. "Just be careful. I don't want to see you get hurt any more than you already are, and I'm afraid you're gonna regret this. When you wake up and realize that friends can't be lovers, you are going to be devastated."

"Let's talk about something else. So, what's in this cake of yours?" Holland asked as she stood and moved to put her empty coffee mug in the dishwasher.

"We'll need some sweetened condensed milk, fresh coconut—"

"Great, why don't you make a list tonight when you get back to your hotel? You can either text it to me or Paris, and we can go pick up the ingredients, or you can get them on your way."

"Oh, I can write them down now if you'd like."

"No, there's no need. It's getting late, and you may not remember, but life on the farm, we get up at the crack of dawn. Besides, I'm sure Paris is dying to go call Asher. Let's let her do that."

I locked eyes with my baby sister and smiled, silently thanking her for getting to the crux of the situation…it was time for Mom to leave. Unfortunately, Mom didn't get the hint and stood in the foyer, holding her purse.

"When did you repaint the interior?"

"Can't remember. Five years ago, or so," Holland answered.

"Those shades, they really need to be changed. I think those are the same ones from when I was here."

"Probably, but they still work." Holland tilted her head and signaled for me to leave, but I couldn't, I didn't want to be rude. So she let out an exasperated breath. "We're going to bed. Mom, let me walk you to your car. Paris, go call Asher." Holland opened the front door, placed one hand on Cora's back, and pushed.

I waited for the front door to close then pulled out my phone. Staring at the black screen, I debated: should I, or shouldn't I? It was definitely should. After all, my life was only going to get worse until I womaned-up and told him how I felt.

So, I called him.

"Paris?"

"Hi. I'm not catching you at a bad time, am I?" I felt like a pre-teen girl and twisted a strand of hair around a finger.

"No, of course not. Are you okay?"

"Yeah, I'm fine. Or rather, I will be."

"What do you mean?" Asher sounded apprehensive.

"I need to talk with you."

"Okay, let's talk."

"No, not over the phone. Can you come over tomorrow?"

"Paris, I don't know."

"Please, Asher. I need to talk to you. It's important to me."

"What about what's important to me?"

"Let me rephrase, it's important to us."

"Then tell me now."

"I can't. I really want to do this in person. Please. Tomorrow. Will you come over tomorrow?"

"Sure, yeah. I have appointments, but I can come after work."

"Asher?"

"Yes?"

"Thank you. I can't tell you how much this means to me."

"I'd do anything for you, you know that."

We disconnected, and for the first time in ten days, I slept.

ASHER

I yawned for the fourth time in as many minutes, then stared at the dashboard clock in my truck. It was only seven-thirty, and I had appointments until four. I had no clue how in the hell I was supposed to concentrate when all I could do was think about Paris and whatever the hell she wanted to talk about.

I let out another yawn.

After I'd hung up, I'd lain in bed wide awake as every possible reason why she might want to talk to me ran through my mind. Her wanting to talk to me about "us" could have meant a thousand and one different things, most of which were bad, a few were tolerable, and one was ideal.

My and Ellie's first stop of the day was at the Sloans' farm, where I checked on two new foals. Then we headed over to the Hightowers', who had several goats. The crazy thing was, they'd never intended to own goats, but when the unclaimed animals kept finding their way onto the property, they decided they better get them checked out regularly.

I was just pulling out of Mr. Howard's driveway after

having given the Great Pyrenees, Captain, another anti-inflammatory injection when I turned to Ellie.

"I've been going nuts all day wondering what she wants to talk about." Ellie, to her credit, didn't roll her eyes at me. The poor woman had been a good sport about my need to talk incessantly about Paris.

"What do you think she wants to talk about? Are you sure she didn't give you any hints at all?"

"I'm positive. She didn't say anything other than she wanted to talk to me in person. She was so damn cryptic, the only clue I got was, *it's important to us.*" I flexed my fingers and rolled my neck, the stress of the last two weeks taking its toll on me.

"You think she's finally come to her senses?" Ellie had asked me this a dozen times already, and each time I answered the same way.

"I don't know, but the wait is killing me."

"Want me to rearrange your appointments?"

"Would you do that? I know I'm not paying you, but I'm dying to go see her."

"Of course I will. I'm a sucker for a happy ending. Can I just rearrange them for any open spots you have?" Ellie opened my appointment book and flipped to this week's calendar.

"Yeah, I have a late start on Thursday, so you can move most to then."

"Will do."

I pulled up the drive to Reid's home, and Ellie jumped out. "Oh, and Asher?"

"Yes?"

"Stay calm. Let her talk first. Make her work a little bit for it, okay?"

I nodded and then drove down the street to Paris's house. Though, when I pulled up her driveway, all the anticipation and anxiousness melted to disappointment.

Her car was nowhere in sight, so I sent her a text.

ME: Got done early. Just got to your house.

Paris: Go on in, Cora should be there. Just leaving grocery store, will be there soon.

HAVING MISSED BEING at the Kelly home and this feeling of welcome that seemed to surround the area, I walked up the steps and went inside without knocking. The Kelly home had always been as familiar as my own. I froze at the sound of a grunt coming from London's office and headed down the hallway, stopping in front of the slightly ajar door.

Cora was lifting tops off banker boxes and rummaging through files of old papers, putting each box back before searching the next. She'd obviously been in here a while, since it looked like she was about halfway through the stack, which was about seven boxes.

Leaning against the doorway, I cleared my throat and glared as Cora startled, scattering papers everywhere. "Something I could help you find?"

"I'm just doing stuff for the girls."

"In London's office?"

"Why are you in here?" Cora asked. "I didn't hear you knock on the front door or ring the bell."

"I've never knocked, I've always just come in, but Paris knows I'm here and told me to come straight in."

"Paris is back?" Cora looked concerned and picked up her pace as she stacked papers back into the last box she'd been searching.

"She's almost back. She was on her way when I texted her.

Clearly, you're in a hurry to, what was it? Help the girls? I'm more than happy to help as well."

"No. I don't need your help. In fact, we don't need you. Why don't you go home, and Paris can just call you when she's ready?"

"No, thanks, I'd rather wait." I crossed my feet at the ankles and continued to lean against the doorframe. "So, what was it you said you were looking for?"

"I didn't say because I wasn't looking for anything. I was actually cleaning and knocked the box over. You startled me. I was just putting this away." Cora stood and moved the box back to the stack.

Something about that didn't sit right with me, but I was smart enough to realize that, even though I didn't trust her, this was a very precarious position. If I were to tell Paris her mom was snooping around London's office without any proof of her doing so, it would only force her to choose sides. Since I wasn't positive how Paris felt about me yet, and I wasn't sure how welcome Cora was in the house, I was in a no-win situation.

Unlike Paris, London wasn't exactly meticulous. So, even though I looked for anything else that seemed out of place, I wouldn't have been able to spot it. There were stacks of papers on the desk, her chair was pulled out and turned around, and an accordion file was overflowing. All of this made me smile, because although London and Paris looked so much alike, this chaos would have given Paris hives. Hell, the woman alphabetized her spice cabinet. I learned that the hard way when I offered to help put away the groceries one time.

I turned at the sound of the front door and smiled as Paris carried in bags of groceries. "Is there more in your Jeep?" I walked over, took the bags from her, and brought them into the kitchen.

"No, just these. What were you doing in London's office?"

"Talking to Cora. She says that she's dusting, but the crazy thing is, she doesn't have any dust rags."

"Cora? She's in—" Paris shut up, and I halted, both of us turning to see Cora bent over and moaning. "Mom? Mom, are you okay? Do you need me to call 911?"

"No, I'm just dizzy, I think I stood too fast. I was doing some dusting, just trying to help, but I haven't eaten much today. That's all, I'm sure."

That was . . . interesting, but I pressed my lips together and waited.

"Here, come over here and sit down. I'll fix you something. We'll make the cake tomorrow. You just rest."

"No. I want us to make it. That's important to you."

Paris threw some stuff together and popped it into the microwave. When it was ready, she set it in front of Cora. "No, it's more important that you eat something. Besides, Asher is here, and he and I really need to talk."

"Can he come back later? I was really looking forward to teaching you that recipe. When you said you wanted to learn something from me and my family, it meant the world to me."

"I do want to learn. It means a lot, it really does. But—" Paris's words were cut off again.

"Oooh. Maybe you're right. I don't feel so good." Cora moaned, and I could practically feel my eyes rolling into the back of my head.

You have to be fucking kidding me. She isn't even a good actress.

"Come on, Mom, let me help you. You can lie down in London's room."

"No. I don't want to be back there."

"Okay, you can lie down in my room."

"No. I just don't want to be back there all alone."

"You won't be, I'll be right here. I promise."

"You promise that you'll stay with me? I feel like such a burden."

So, you're going to make her stay with you and wait on you, to what? Ease that burden?

"Oh, wait. You and Asher were going to talk." Cora grabbed her head and slowly massaged her temples. "Let me grab my purse. I'll be back tomorrow." She rested one hand on Paris's upper arm and swayed back and forth. "I'm just going to head up to my hotel."

"You have to be fucking kidding me," I said, a bit too loudly.

"Asher, that was rude."

"Paris, I came over because you asked me to."

"I understand that, but shit happens. We can rearrange our time. I'll call you. My mom needs me right now."

"I thought it was important. I rearranged my day."

"I appreciate that, I really do, but at that time I had no clue my mom was going to get sick. We need to talk, and we will, I promise."

I turned my focus to Cora, whose expression held just the barest hint of satisfaction.

Needless to say, I was stunned, in utter disbelief. How the hell was Paris buying this? I'd never thought she was naïve, but maybe I was the one who was being naïve and the only *us* she wanted to talk about was us going back to being friends.

* * *

MONDAY MORNING, I swung by and picked up Ellie, who started in almost immediately with the questions. "So, how did everything go yesterday?"

"Don't ask."

"Uh oh, what happened?"

"Her mom is what happened. Her mom did not want us alone, so she pretended to be sick."

"Are you sure? That's pretty juvenile."

"I'm positive."

"And Paris bought it?"

"Hook, line, and sinker. She brushed me off and told me we would talk another day. I think I made yesterday out to be more than it was going to be."

Ellie looked thoughtful, but instead of saying anything else, she settled back against her seat and stayed silent for the rest of the drive. I put on my blinker and turned into the driveway of my next client.

"Oh, look." Ellie pointed at the Cavalier King Charles Spaniel running toward the truck. "Shit, he's going to run out of the gate."

"No, he won't. That's Charlie. Watch."

"Charlie? Not too original, huh?"

"Nope. And we're here to see his sister, Sammy." I pulled forward over the cattle guard and opened my truck door. Charlie jumped up and into my lap. He hopped onto my center console, ready to ride the rest of the way to his house with me.

"Hello, Charlie. You obviously aren't one of those dogs that's afraid of the vet, huh?" Ellie asked as she rubbed behind his ears.

We parked then made our way to the front door, Charlie circling around my feet to ensure that I went nowhere else and that he was the one to announce my presence to his mom.

Ellie let out a laugh. "Sammy. We're here to see Sammy the Samoyed, sister of Charlie the King Charles. Got it."

Sammy waddled over, excited to see me. I looked up and waved to the mom, standing in the open doorway. "Morning, Patty."

"Hey, Asher, who do we have here?"

"This is Ellie, she's a vet tech and is going to start helping me."

"Okay, just come on in when you're done."

"Will do." I waved again before heading to the bed of my truck to lower the tailgate. I pressed the side button, and a platform similar to a wheelchair lift lowered to the ground.

"So, what are we checking out today?"

"Sammy had knee surgery, and we are just making sure everything is healing properly so we can remove the stitches."

"Did you do it?"

"No. It's actually the only thing I don't handle in the practice. I have two different veterinarians who I refer clients to and who refer clients to me when they need to."

When we were done, I cleaned up in Patty's washroom, then we were on our way.

"Asher, I love this setup. I've always thought about grooming and how much fun it would be to be a mobile groomer."

"You should. I know a ton of clients who would love having a mobile groomer."

"I'm going to do some research when I get home. But I would truly love it."

"Then you should do it."

"Don't give up." Ellie totally changed the subject.

"What?"

"Don't give up on Paris. If you love her, then she's worth fighting for. Give her some time."

"I've given her time. Hell, we've been out of high school for ten years. I don't know that she's ever actually, seriously dated anyone. I always just assumed we were waiting for each other, you know? I always knew that I was going to veterinary school, and that would be eight years, add that to losing my dad, then her dad getting sick and then losing him, it seemed that it was never the right time." I kept my eyes on the winding country road. "If we ever needed a date to something, we called each other. I always thought it was us and we were just waiting for the right time. I'm not sure there is such a thing as the right time, though, at least not for us."

"Answer me this, then. If you knew she was going to wake up and realize you were the one, how long are you willing to wait?"

And just like that, I knew my answer . . . indefinitely. I'd wait forever for Paris.

PARIS

I threw one arm over my face, exhausted. What a day. Between working myself up to talk to Asher, Mom's dizzy spell, and then Asher leaving upset, god, it was crazy.

"What?" I answered the knock at my door without sitting up.

"How did yesterday go?" London asked.

"Don't ask."

"Why, what happened?" This time, it was Holland who spoke.

Sitting up, I saw the quizzical faces of both my sisters, who were standing at the foot of my bed. I loved that even in this chaos, where I felt as if my world was falling apart, two constants remained. My sisters truly were my best friends.

I grabbed one of my throw pillows and hugged it to my chest. "So . . . this is what happened . . ." I told them everything, beginning with Mom getting dizzy, Asher leaving pissed off before I had a chance to talk to him, me stressed out because I was still worried about her and worried that

Asher would never give me a chance to explain, and freaking out about everything Mom had said. If they weren't worn out when I was done, they had some serious problems.

"So, what are you going to do?" London asked as she cradled her baby close.

"I was going to talk with both of you about Mom."

"Not about Cora. I don't want to talk about her because, frankly, I don't care. What are you going to do about Asher?"

"I'm going to try again even though Mom thinks it's a bad idea. She thinks he's too demanding and that there is something going on between him and Ellie."

"Bullshit," London spat out. "You heard that voicemail. We all did. There is nothing going on between them."

"Yeah, I'm going to side with London on this one. When I found out that she was Dick Brooks's sister, I about died, but it makes sense."

"Was she also a dick?" I asked Holland, since I had no idea what she was insinuating.

"No, I meant about her helping him. As much as I hate to admit it and would never do it in front of the asshole, he knows a lot about horses and animals. If she's anything like him, then she's really only interested in helping Asher at work."

"But what about their chemistry? Mom said there was a spark."

London groaned, and I noted that her lips had turned white, as if she were pinching them together, fighting the urge to say something. Please not now, I didn't have time to deal with London's temper or Holland's attitude.

"The only spark I saw was when I thought Asher was going to smack her. That was, of course, right after he smacked me. I'm telling you . . . he looked at her like a sister." Holland was adamant.

"I've had it, Cora needs to keep her fucking mouth shut and her nose out of our business. She's been gone all our lives, but the second she comes back, she's what? The holy grail of motherly knowledge? No. She screwed up her life and her own relationship, and now she's trying to screw up yours. I refuse to let her do that. If you mess this up, then it will be because you don't want him, not because she's talking shit. Paris, you know you love that man, and he's crazy about you. I have no idea why you're even listening to Cora, but stop. Hell, stop letting her come over."

"She is just trying to make up for lost time. I don't think she means any harm, I truly think she is only trying to help."

"And I think that you're delusional. Regardless, call Asher."

"Okay, I'll call him in just a minute. But while I have you both here, I wanted to ask you about something." I was biting my fingernails, which was a horrid habit but one I did when I was nervous. I clenched my hands into fists. "I've already thought this through, and maybe now isn't the right time, but . . ."

"Why do I have a feeling I'm not going to like this?" London groaned.

"I want to talk with you about Mom moving in here. If she's moving back, there's no sense in her staying at a hotel."

"No. Absolutely not." London stood, already backing away from me and blocking out the conversation.

"London, I think something's wrong with her. You didn't see her yesterday. She could barely walk. She's already missed out on so much, the least we can do is give her some time."

"And why did she miss out? Because she left. She left. Not Dad. Her. It was her choice. If she wasn't in love with Dad anymore, then why didn't she just move out and get a house in Orlando or something? Not somewhere else, where we never saw her again. Millions of people get divorced, but they don't divorce their children, it isn't normal."

"But what if she's telling the truth and Dad didn't want her to see us?" I searched for an ounce of compassion in London but found none. "How about you, Holland? What do you think?"

"I don't know. Honestly, I don't feel anything either way. You all forget, I was three when she left. She is nothing more than a person in stories and a face in photographs. She's a stranger to me."

"Then she needs to be here, so you can at least get to know her."

"I know her, Dad made sure that we knew her. He kept her photos up and told me that I was like her."

"Yeah, he told me that as well," London cut in. "But he only said that to make us feel that she was always with us, he didn't mean it. He was being a good father. Hell, none of us is anything like that woman. Thank god."

I couldn't believe what I was hearing. How could my own sisters feel this way?

"Let me ask you this, Paris. If she wrote all the time like she says, where are the letters?"

"She said Dad returned them."

"And does that sound like something Dad would do? He told us we were like her, and he kept her photos up. Our entire lives, he always . . . always did what was best for us, and it didn't matter how hard it was for him. Dad never kept us away from checking the mail. In fact, I can't remember him ever actually being the one to walk down to the mailbox. So you tell me how he hid all those letters she sent us."

I didn't have an answer, so I stayed silent.

"Let's say by some act of magic, he did. What about after he died? She said that she tried to reach him. Have you seen any letters? Have you taken any phone calls? We kept his cell phone number for a *year*. There weren't any calls. So, tell me, how did she try to reach him? Ouija board? If so, then she knew he was dead."

I cringed. "I don't know. But we have time to find out. She needs us, and that is all that matters to me. We don't have much family left, and I'm not willing to take a chance on losing any more if I can help it."

"We have all the family that matters, but fine, I'll leave it to you two to decide, since you'll have to live with her anyway. I'm against it, though."

I watched London leave before turning my focus on Holland. "Be honest, what do you want?"

"I'm okay with whatever you decide. Trust your gut, it'll never lie. This is your house."

"It's yours too."

"I know that, but that isn't what I meant. I'm always out in the stables, I come in to eat and sleep, that's about it. You are here and will have to be with her, so I think this is up to you." Holland headed toward my bedroom door. "I'm going to go jump in the shower. Night, Par."

"Night, Holl."

Once the door was closed behind her, I squeezed my pillow tighter and pondered what the hell I was going to do. First things first, I was going to call Asher.

"Hello?"

It was *not* Asher.

"Oh, I'm sorry, I think I dialed the wrong number."

"Are you looking for Asher?"

"Yeah. But I can call back another time." My heart was racing, and everything in me was screaming that the woman on the phone was Ellie, even though I'd only heard her speak once, for a few seconds.

117

"No, hold on. I think I just heard him come out of the shower."

Is she trying to be helpful?

Mom had been right. Asher had come here yesterday, then went right back and crawled into bed with her. I clutched at my chest as I felt something inside it shatter into pieces. I could feel each individual shard slicing up my insides, digging deeper and deeper and making my soul bleed. Some were sharp, some were jagged, and some broke in such a way that they refracted light. A light that had been my hope for a future with Asher, but slowly . . . so slowly, those pieces were being swept up and away.

"Paris? Paris, are you there?"

I shook my head when Asher's voice came on the line. "Yeah, I'm here. I'm sorry to disturb you. We can talk tomorrow."

"Wait. Don't hang up. What'd you need?"

"Oh, nothing. Just wanted to try to . . . I just . . . I miss—"

"Hold on, Paris." I was shocked by Asher cutting me off. Then I realized he was cutting me off to talk to someone else. "I'll be right there," Asher said to the woman whose voice I'd never forget.

"Was that Ellie?"

"Yeah. I got a late call, so I called Ellie, and she wanted to come. When we got back, she offered to make dinner before she headed home."

"I don't want to keep you, it seems like you're busy. I'm sorry to have interrupted."

"Paris, what is up with the wounded-puppy act? You turned me down, remember? Then I came over, like a glutton for punishment, and you brushed me off."

"I'm just confused."

"Well, I wish you'd figure it out, because you're dragging

me along your emotional rollercoaster. I told you how I feel, and that hasn't changed."

"Really?" I wanted to shout bullshit, like London had done earlier.

"Yes, really. Why would you ask such a thing?"

"Oh, I don't know. Call me crazy, but I have a hard time understanding how someone who claims to have been—"

"Not have been . . . am." Asher's voice was broken.

"Claims to *have been* in love with someone for most of their life can move on to the next woman so fast. I don't know, seems sort of mind blowing to me." I knew I was lashing out at him by putting emphasis on the words he'd just corrected, but damn it, I was hurting, so he should too.

"Move on? What? You mean because I accepted help? For your information—no, you know what, I'm not going to explain myself. I shouldn't have to. Two weeks ago, I offered you my world in exchange for your heart, and you rejected me. That was the moment you lost all input in my life. You don't have a right to question me about anything I'm doing. And if you don't trust me, or if you think so little of me, then everything is just how it should be. I love you, but I'm not going to allow you to play games with me."

"I'm not playing games."

"Really? Because it sure seems like you are. What? You don't want me, but no one else can have me either? Is that it, Paris? No one would have treated you better than I would have, no one would have loved you more."

Silence filled the line, and I fought back the tears. God, was that what he thought? That I looked at him like a shiny toy I didn't want anyone else to play with? "Asher, I'm sorry."

Nothing.

Just dead silence. I pulled my phone from my ear and looked at the screen. It was black.

He'd hung up on me.

Asher James Kinkaide had hung up on me.

I dropped my phone onto my bed before kicking off my boots and walking over to my window. The hum from the overhead ceiling fan was soothing to my tired soul. I stared out and over toward Asher's house. When we were kids, we used to use flashlights to signal each other, then we would sneak out and meet halfway. I thought we were so cool and secretive. I laughed at the memory, then felt a sense of comfort when I remembered my daddy finally confessing he used to watch me walk through the pasture, just to make sure I was okay. He never worried about me, though. He knew Asher would never allow anything bad to happen to me.

Leaning forward, I rested my forehead against the foggy pane, the only evidence of the temperature difference. It was still warm outside, but in my room, it was cool.

I'm not okay anymore, Daddy.

Asher won't protect me this time. I wiped the tears from my face. How could he, when he was the one who was hurting me? I let out a deep breath, knowing that I deserved every bit of ire that Asher threw my way.

Before pulling my shades down for the evening, I wondered for the briefest moment if Asher was looking out his window, or if he was looking at Ellie.

* * *

I HAD JUST TAKEN a pan of biscuits out of the oven when I heard a cough behind me. Twirling, I was shocked to see Wally standing there.

"Morning, Wally, want a biscuit?"

"Don't mind if I do. Is London here?"

"Not yet, but she should be any moment. Is there something I can help you with?"

"No. I just wanted to say hey and let her know that I was back from vacation."

"Oh, okay. Just have a seat. Want some coffee?"

Wally held up his thermos to show he'd come equipped, just like every day for as long as I could remember.

"So tell me, what did you and Anne do?" Wally and his wife Anne had been like a second set of parents to us growing up. I set the butter onto the table then snagged my phone to send London a text to let her know Wally was here, but she beat me to it by walking in at that moment with Holland on her heels. That wasn't uncommon, since they both worked the pasture in the morning.

Wally stood. Even though he was a rugged old ranch hand, he was still a Southern gentleman, and as such, he stood when a lady walked into the room. "Morning, London, Holland."

"Hi, Wally, welcome back. We hope that your vacation was great."

"It was, thank you. I was just getting ready to tell Paris about Mount Rushmore."

"Is that where you went?" London slid into a seat opposite him, and Holland took a seat at the end of the table.

"Yep, it was our first vacation with the whole family. Both of our daughters went, plus their husbands and the grandkids."

"I know that you and Anne must have been in heaven having the kids with you," I stated.

"We were." Wally shoved the rest of the biscuit into his mouth. "Well, I'll get to work."

"Hold up, Wally, I'd like to talk with you about something." London chewed on her bottom lip. She was clearly nervous about whatever was on her mind.

Wally leaned back into the chair. "Is everything okay? You look a little stressed."

London folded her hands and rested them on the table. "Yes, everything is fine." She waited a few seconds, then recanted her statement. "Well, no, not really."

Wally was genuinely confused as he asked, "What's going on, London?"

"Cora, that's what's going on."

"What about her?"

"She's back."

I felt as if I was watching a tennis match, the back and forth between the two of them.

"She showed up here while you were gone and said you told her about Dad and about Tera."

Wally's face went pale. "London, I'm sorry, but it was what your father asked me to do."

"Daddy asked you to talk to her?" I interrupted, wanting Wally to talk more about Dad's final wishes.

"Yeah. He told me that she'd probably call someday looking for him. I was to tell her that he was gone, how you three were doing, and that she'd missed her chance."

"Missed her chance for what?" London asked.

"No clue, that was all he said. I was assuming missed her chance to get to know you three. I had no clue she'd actually show up here. Why now?"

"That's what I'd like to figure out." London tilted her head and stared at me.

"What?" I threw up my hands. "I don't know what she wants. I think she just wants to get to know us."

I groaned when Wally and London shared a look.

"Wally, you're the closest thing we have to a father now. Please don't share anything about us with anyone." London was hurt. I'm not sure that she'd be as hurt if it would have been anyone else.

"London, I want to respect your wishes, and from here on out, I will. But that was one of the final things your father asked of me, and if you want to fire me over it, then so be it. But I feel as though I did right by your dad."

London grabbed hold of Wally's wrinkled hands. I studied the two; London's were smooth, whereas his were callused. A person's hands revealed a lot about their journey in life. "No one is getting fired. I'm glad you did what Daddy asked."

ASHER

The rest of my week sucked. Paris never tried to call again, and I was too upset to try to call her. But fuck it, I was in such a bad mood that I decided to tell Ellie I needed a few days alone. My story probably sounded more like a country song than it did anything else . . . just a man with a broken heart all alone in his pickup truck. Yeah, I could hear it.

I was thinking about said song when I turned into the Elbow Room and then found myself sitting back in my spot, drinking a pint of Yuengling.

"Hey, you're getting to be one of my best patrons. Well, you would be if you actually paid," Marcus said. "What's on your mind today? Still Paris?"

"Yes and no."

"Start with the no, please. I'm sick of hearing about Paris."

I punched him in the arm. "That's okay, I'm sick of talking about her. Have you met Cora?"

"I know she's back, but I haven't seen her. London is pissed."

"Why? I thought they were all happy to have their mom back."

Marcus scoffs and gives me an incredulous look. "Not London. She thinks Cora is up to something, and according to her, Holland is pretty damn indifferent."

"Oh, the woman is up to something, all right."

"Why would you say that? Have you talked to her?"

"The other day when I went by, she was in London's office going through old boxes of paperwork. When I asked her what she was doing, she lied. She had no idea that I had been watching her for a good five minutes before that."

"What did Paris say when you told her?"

"I didn't get a chance to. As soon as she got home, Cora started acting all sick and demanding that Paris not leave her side. We were supposed to talk. Needless to say, that was fucked."

"You think she faked it to keep you from talking to Paris about it?"

"I definitely think she faked it. Whether that was the reason, or she just doesn't want us together, I don't know."

"I never thought I'd say this, but that house seems to be all drama."

The thought of stepping away from the Kelly sisters was disheartening, and I could tell by the grief that crossed Marcus's face that he felt the same way. "But that's what bothers me most, it never used to be. Not until Cora came back."

"Are you sure? Didn't you and Paris stop talking before Cora showed up?" He held up a finger before walking around the wall that divided the dining area from the kitchen and coming back with a basket of fries.

"It isn't the same. Paris was just shocked, that was all. I think she would have come to her senses and come around."

I stopped talking when the door to the bar opened and Braden walked in.

"Hey, you two." He waved at both of us.

"Just get off shift?"

He didn't really need to answer, since his green Seminole County Sheriff's Department uniform did so for him. "Yeah, I was headed home when I saw your truck out front, so I thought I'd stop by. Got a few?"

I nodded. So much for my peace and quiet. I sincerely hoped Braden didn't get all fucking girly and want to talk about feelings and Paris.

"Can I get you something to drink or eat?" Marcus asked.

"Just a water, thanks. Not going to be long, London's making dinner."

"Wow, since when does London cook?"

"Since Cora showed up and London started avoiding the big house." Braden took the glass from Marcus. "I have a feeling it is only going to get worse."

"Why's that?" I matched Braden's movements, but I was drinking a beer instead. I didn't have anyone to rush home to.

"Paris has decided to ask Cora to move in."

I almost choked. "She what?"

"I guess the girls talked about it and they left it up to Paris to decide, since she's at the house more than anyone else. Anyway, Cora has been staying at the La Quinta over by the university."

I couldn't decide whether that news was the hammer or the nail, but whichever it was, it was sealing my future with Paris shut. "Is that why you stopped by? To tell me this?"

"No. I stopped by to ask for your help."

"My help? With what?"

"The girls are going to go through their dad's old room tomorrow and clean it out. No one has been in there since

Samuel died. Anyway, they are going to make it up for Cora. I wanted to know if you were free to help me move some furniture."

I let out a long, drawn-out sigh, because tomorrow was Saturday and my only day off this week. I also didn't want to do anything that would bring Cora and Paris closer together.

"Before you say no, London wants you there. She thinks we'll find something when we're cleaning out his room."

"What?"

"Not sure, some missing piece. Whatever it is that Cora is back for. She's been going through London's office when no one is around—"

"London knows?"

"She suspects. Wait. You know for certain?" Braden's eyes were wide with surprise.

"Yeah, I caught her. But I didn't get to tell anyone because that was the day she suddenly got sick and I was pushed out so she could *rest*."

"Then I take it you'll help?" Braden asked.

"Damn right, I'll help."

I was going to ask Marcus, but he was on the phone.

"You don't mind? Thanks. I owe you," Marcus said, then disconnected before turning to smile at us. "I'm going to help too. I'm tired of our own little dysfunctional family being divided. I kind of liked knowing where to go for food."

I laughed. "Do we want more help? I can ask Reid. He really is a nice guy."

"Sure, I'm always up for ruining Holland's day," Braden said and laughed.

"Yep, you're family, all right. She just endears herself to being picked on," I agreed.

* * *

At seven o'clock the next morning, I pulled in front of the Kelly house.

Get out of the truck, Asher, you're a grown-ass man. What the hell are you doing just sitting here? Okay, mental talks weren't my strong suit, but determination was.

I got out and walked up the three steps to the front door, which opened before I even had a chance to knock.

"Morning, Kitten." I leaned down to kiss her on her cheek, just like I had done for years, and froze midway. Fuck. She wasn't my Kitten, and we weren't in that type of relationship anymore, where I would give her a peck. Maybe being here wasn't such a great idea. I righted myself. "Sorry. Old habit, hard to break. But I will." I walked past her, and if I wasn't mistaken, I heard her whisper.

"Don't."

I took a deep breath, every instinct in me wanting to turn around, sweep her into my arms, and kiss her until she admitted that she was madly in love with me. I paused for a moment and took her in.

"It feels like it's been forever since I've seen you." Her words were soft, and she sounded sort of broken.

I tilted my head slightly and decided to keep the banter going for as long as she was willing to play. I stuck a finger in my left ear and wiggled it around, pretending to clear out my ear canal. "Did I hear wrong, or did someone actually admit that she missed me?"

"You wish," she scoffed, rolling her eyes. "You totally need to get your hearing checked."

"Sure. Okay, whatever you say." I pursed my lips together, not believing for one second that I'd heard her wrong, then turned to head toward the master wing.

I'd only been in Samuel's room twice. The first time was when I was a kid playing Hide and Go Seek with the girls, and second time was when I asked him for Paris's hand . . . I couldn't think about that. Whatever. Still, it was the last time I was in there, and I was so nervous that I hadn't realized that everything was exactly as it had been when I was a child.

Well, almost exactly: Reid was a new addition.

"You're early, I didn't see your truck out front," I greeted Reid, who had a screwdriver in his hand and was removing a bracket from a wall that had hung curtains.

"I walked over."

"Just start on anything," Braden hollered. I couldn't see him or where he was, so I stepped deeper into the room and found him removing stuff from the top of Samuel's closet. "London is feeding the baby, but then she'll be in here to direct. Holland is taking care of the horses, and I'm not sure where Paris is. Anyway, they've decided they want everything out. Paris went and bought some paint." Braden didn't get down from the ladder as he caught me up. He just dropped another stack of jeans onto the floor to join the rest he'd already thrown down.

Since Braden seemed to have that under control, I started removing drawers from the cabinets, so we could get the piece out without breaking our backs. "Where's all this furniture going?" I asked as I slid the first nightstand away from the wall.

"We're going to move it out to the porch and then take it to one of the back rooms over in the stables. Holland wants to strip it and refinish it, since it's well-made," Braden said.

"Is that your way of saying it's heavy as shit?" I asked, worried since I'd only just begun, and that was with the smallest piece.

"Something like that." He chuckled.

I pulled out more drawers and stacked them on the bed. By the time I was done, there were fifteen drawers stacked in the middle of the king-sized, four-post bed.

Reid had also finished, so the two of us moved the chest of drawers out, then the nightstands, followed by the dresser.

When we returned, Paris was there. Actually, I smelled Paris before I saw her. She had always reminded me of sunshine and honey—sweet and warm at the same time. Peaches? Or maybe it was orange blossoms. She was sitting on the bed and going through the items that had been in the drawers, dividing them into piles. Every so often, I'd glance over, and she'd have a wide smile on her lips as she held something of her father's, like his old gray flannel shirt that was threadbare. She looked as if she was on the verge of crying as she flipped through old cards that she and her sisters had made for him when they were growing up. He'd kept everything. Some people thought Samuel Kelly was tough, but those three girls were his world.

I knew I was wrong the moment I did it, but I couldn't help it, this was Paris. My Paris, and she was hurting. All I could think of was how could I ease her pain. Cupping her face, I lifted it and gazed into her dark amber eyes. "He's right here, P, he never left you."

She nodded and pressed her cheek tighter to my palm, so I was holding more of her face without breaking our eye contact.

I wasn't sure how long we had stood there, but when I followed Paris's eyes to the side and noticed Holland, Braden, Reid, and London all staring at us, I figured it had been longer than I'd realized.

"Keep going, don't let us stop you," Holland said.

"I liked seeing you two make mooney-eyes," London added.

Paris pulled back and righted herself. Our moment was totally broken.

"Fine, you two might as well get back to work, then,"

Holland said as she tossed a roll of large garbage bags onto the bed.

I returned to work, and Paris returned to sorting, but all morning, it was like an electric current was in the air. I could feel every time Paris's eyes were on me, the hairs on my arms would stand up and I would look over, only to lock eyes with the most beautiful woman I'd ever seen.

And whatever was going on with me, the feeling must have been reciprocated, because every time I got lost admiring the way the sun kissed her skin, she glanced up and caught me.

Just before lunch, Paris left the room, and her absence was immediately a dark cloud over what had been a bright day. When she hollered for us to come eat, I grinned like an idiot. I was still grinning as London, Holland, and Braden took their seats, leaving me the one right next to Paris.

I shook my head and winked at Holland when I realized that the only other person not sitting was Reid. "Wow, I get to sit by two beautiful women. The question is, which two will I choose? I can have London on my right and Paris on my left. Or I can have Holland on my left and Paris on my right. Hmmm, decisions, decisions."

Holland's face turned red the moment she caught on. Yep, either way I'd be next to Paris, but she was the one who was going to be screwed. Because if I didn't take the seat next to her, then it only left Reid.

I sat between Paris and London and locked eyes with Holland.

She let out a growl when Reid sat next to her.

"You okay there, tiger?" Reid quietly asked Holland, which only made her growl louder.

"Where's Marcus? I thought he said he was coming to help?" Braden asked as we passed around the plates of food.

"He is, actually, he should be here any time. He had to

close last night, which means he didn't get out of there until four." I grabbed a roll just as the front door opened, and in walked Marcus. "Speak of the devil."

"And the devil shall appear," Holland finished for me, but she was glaring at Marcus. I turned to see why, and my stomach dropped.

Shit, this wasn't good. This wasn't good at all. Why in the hell was Ellie with him? Sure, I'd like her and Paris to get to know each other, but first, I had to convince Paris that there was nothing between us.

"Look who I found walking down the road." Marcus pointed to Ellie.

"And why didn't you leave her?" Holland mumbled.

"Hi. Sorry to interrupt. I didn't mean to." Ellie gave a half-wave. "But Marcus kept insisting and wouldn't let me finish my walk."

"No interruption at all." London stood. "Braden . . ." But she didn't even have to finish the sentence, because he was already up and grabbing two more chairs while London was getting two more plates and glasses.

"Here, Ellie, you can sit next to your brother." Holland stood and grabbed her plate.

"No, I'm putting her right down here. You stay seated. You've been working so hard today." London batted her eyelashes, and I fought back my smirk.

Fuck you, Holland mouthed.

I lost it. I couldn't stop laughing. This was the most clusterfuck lunch I'd ever had at this table, and it was so emotionally strained that it would be a miracle if we all made it out alive. I wouldn't be shocked if someone sprinkled someone else's food with some anthrax, that was, of course, if we just happened to have anthrax lying around. I wouldn't put it past Holland, though.

"So, Ellie, are you here to stay, or are you just visiting

your brother?" London passed the food over to Marcus and Ellie.

"I'm here to stay. I'm going through a divorce."

"I'm sorry to hear that."

"Don't be . . ." Ellie was explaining to them about Lance, but I was focused on Paris. She hadn't said a word since Ellie walked in, and her demeanor had changed. A few hours ago, I had knocked down the walls we had put up against each other, but hers was back up, and she was safely tucked behind it once again.

That didn't work for me.

So, I slid a hand over to her lap and lightly squeezed. For the first time in weeks, I felt my heart start beating again. I hadn't realized it had stopped. That was, I hadn't realized until Paris wove her finger between mine and held on.

After lunch, we became a well-oiled machine, and I was pleased to see the girls had warmed up to Ellie and she was staying to help. London, Holland, and Ellie were stationed in the living room, which was where we were stacking boxes for the girls to separate into trash, save, or donate piles. Hangers full of clothes were draped over chairs, and the contents of his dresser drawers were in a heap, ready to be divided. Paris was in his bathroom, tossing out his old medicines and toiletries and giving the occasional order on how we, the guys, should be doing things.

"What are we doing with his old mattress and box springs?" I asked as I leaned into the bathroom.

Paris was holding her dad's bottle of cologne and sniffing it, tears pooling in her eyes. Her tears were going to break me today. I wrapped my arms around her from behind and propped my chin in the crook of her shoulder. "You're so fucking beautiful."

She met my eyes in the mirror's reflection, and in them, I found my answers. Yeah, I was going to fight for this, for us. I squeezed her tight and placed a few kisses on her neck just behind her ear.

"Oh god, that feels so good," she moaned.

"Later." I placed another quick kiss on her neck. I gave her a wicked grin, because she looked just as dazed as I was. "First, I need to know what you want us to do with the bed."

"We're tossing it. That thing is so old, it's probably the same mattress he had before Mom left."

"In other words, it's the mattress you were conceived on," I teased.

Paris threw her hands over her ears. "God, don't say that. You'll make me lose my lunch. Clorox. I need bleach for my ears. I'm still hearing you say that, ugh."

I chuckled, then headed back out to start dismantling the bed, but Braden and Marcus had beaten me to it and were already lifting the mattress. What was under it made me freeze.

"Paris, come here, please."

Braden and Marcus had their hands full trying to balance the mattress and get it out of the room, so I turned to Reid. "Will you get Holland and London?" My voice was calm when I really wanted to scream. I would have, too, had London not chewed us all out thirty minutes ago for being so loud, we woke Tera up.

PARIS

There was a stack of letters, tied with a shoestring, sitting on the box spring.

"What's wrong?" Holland raced in, London close behind.

"Letters. Dad kept letters." My voice was softer than I had intended, but I was somewhat in shock. My dad had always been gentle with us, but I'd just never imagined him being sentimental.

"Who are they from?" London asked as she stepped forward and looked over my shoulder.

"I don't know." I reached forward and picked up the stack. They were flattened from years under the weight of the mattress. Thumbing the corners of the envelopes, I looked at the return addresses on them. "It looks like they are all between Mom and Dad."

"But I thought she said he returned all her letters?" London asked, looking ready to tell me that she told me so.

"Obviously not, if they're there," Holland pointed out.

"Do you three want to stay in here to read them? We can leave," Asher offered, and I reached out to stop him.

"No. Stay. We're all family. We have no secrets. Let's take these to the table."

We stayed back as everyone filed out of the room. On one hand, I felt as if so many questions about the past were about to be answered, but on the other, I felt a strange calmness come over me, a resolve, where past and present met. I guessed I was about to find out if I had been a fool, or if I had been right to hold out hope.

When Asher and I reached the door, he slid his strong arm around my shoulders, pulling me against his side as we walked to the kitchen. No matter what the letters revealed, I felt safe. Asher pulled out my chair and waited for me to sit, immediately going into protection mode.

"You three read. I'll make some coffee."

Marcus and Braden had come back in, and Reid and Asher were catching them up on what happened. I ignored them and tugged the shoelace free before fanning the letters out across the table. "Look at these dates." Holland and London leaned forward on their elbows so they could see. "They span the entire twenty-two years she was gone."

"That isn't very many for twenty-two years," London pointed out. "There can't be more than twenty here."

It wasn't, I silently agreed as I picked up the first letter, pulled out the folded piece of stationery, and read.

SAMUEL,

I don't think that it's fair for you to be writing and trying to guilt trip me into coming back. I'm happy where I am. I deserve to be happy. I'm glad to hear that the girls are doing well, but I always knew that you were what was best for them. I'm returning the photos you sent. I'm traveling so much, and I don't want to lose them.

Cora

I SHOOK the envelope and let the enclosed photos drop out. The first one was of the three of us standing in front of the house with our backpacks. Flipping it over, I read: *Holland's first day of school. Paris is now a third grader, and it's London's first day of middle school.* I passed the picture around. "He included our school photos as well." I passed the letter and envelope before moving on to the next.

Pulling the letter and photo out, it was clear that Dad had been hurt or pissed when he wrote it. The pen had been pressed to the paper so hard that the ink bled through in places. "Listen to this one, Dad must have laid into her about something."

"Why do you say that?" London asked.

Flipping the photo back over so they could see, I held it up. "It's one of the ones Dad took every year, you know, on the first day of school on the front porch." In black Sharpie, he'd written in large, bold letters: Big day in the Kelly house. Holland's first day at middle school. Paris's first day of high school, and the beginning of London's senior year. "I hadn't even realized that was a momentous year."

"No, but Daddy had." London took the photo and traced his strong, masculine print with her index finger.

Finally getting to the letter to see what Dad had actually said, I unfolded the stationery and read aloud.

SAMUEL,

Thanks for keeping me updated about the girls, you're doing a great job. Much better than I ever would have. There's no need to send the photos, though. I explain this every time. I'm traveling and seeing the world and have no place to keep them safe. But I do appreciate you always sending me money. Is there any way you could send more?

Cora

UNABLE TO BELIEVE what I was reading or the pure greediness of the woman, I reached for another letter and continued on. Letter after letter, they were almost all the same, Dad ignoring her request and still sending photos, and her sending them back and asking for money at the same time.

"This one's unopened." I held it up. "It was marked 'return to sender.'" After slipping my nail under the edge of the seal, I pulled out the letter and teared up when I realized I was about to read my dad's emotions written out. Cora's writing and emotions hadn't bothered me, but these were going to be my dad's, and I was afraid that he'd gone to his grave still loving her.

CORA,

All three girls are officially women. I don't like the way that sounds. Holland came home sick from school today. When I asked her what was wrong, she wouldn't talk to me. She waited until London got home, and then the three girls were holed up in London's room all night. I let them be, but after going through it with London all by myself, I think I'm sort of a pro.

I wish you'd come see them. London graduates next month, I'll buy you a plane ticket and get you a hotel room if you'd like. You don't even have to let her know you're there if you don't want to. I just think that you will regret it someday if you miss these once-in-a-lifetime moments. Please consider it and let me know. You'd be so impressed with how wonderful they are. I know that I am.

Sam

I GLANCED OVER AT ASHER, whose eyes were soulful. He wasn't passing judgment or saying anything. He was letting me come to my own conclusions.

"Well, we know how this turned out, since the letter wasn't even opened . . . she didn't come. Shocker. Was that the most recent one?" London asked. Then not wanting to dwell on the sadness, she reached for the stack and scanned the postmarks. "No, here's the next." She handed it to me.

My hands were shaking, and a cold chill had broken out across my forehead as I looked back at all the letters from Cora. They were all about Cora. What could Dad give her? Could he give her more money? How happy she was. Didn't she deserve to be happy? Never once did she ask about him, how he was or how he was doing.

I read through letter after letter. There were several times through the years when letters had been returned, and then it would be a year or so before he'd hear from her. When he did, it was always because she was asking for money. I felt so lost because, once again, I'd been so wrong. London saw right through Cora's crap, and I hadn't. I'd bought in to her lies.

Reaching the final letter, I let out a sigh. Going through these had been more of an ordeal than emptying his bedroom had. I was mentally and emotionally drained.

I read the postmark. "This was during Dad's chemo."

141

Samuel,

I'm sorry to hear about your cancer. You're a good man, and I hate this for you. I know that you want me to come to the funeral, but I don't know if I can. Traveling is expensive. I will try to save up and see what I can do. Please leave a little something for me. You know how hard it is for a woman out on her own in the world.

Cora

"What the hell?" I tossed the letter down, fighting my urge to rip it to shreds. "I don't ever want to see her again. All he asked was for her to come to his funeral, and she was asking for more money. What kind of person does that? Daddy was a great man. He did everything for us. We needed snacks for a class party? He made sure we had them. We needed a costume? He'd run us around until we found it. That man treated us better than we deserved, and she . . . she has the nerve to come back here, to his home, for what? What does she want?"

"I don't know." Asher's strong hands tightened around my shoulders as he spoke, his words as comforting as a warm blanket.

I looked at everyone to see if any of them had an answer, and that was when I remembered how not alone we really were. Marcus, Reid, and Ellie were all leaning against the kitchen island, watching with varying degrees of understanding and anger. Even they saw it, and they didn't even know the woman.

I was such an idiot.

"What have I done?"

"What do you mean?" London whispered.

"I trusted her when I should have trusted you. I'm sorry.

I'm so sorry. I can't believe that I was so stupid. How could I have doubted him?"

"Come here." My chair slid out, then Asher was pulling me into his arms. "There is nothing wrong with wanting to believe the best about someone."

"It is wrong when I knew better. My daddy was always such a good man, I knew he'd never be mean to anyone, but I doubted him." I wiped the tears away.

"Paris, Cora has put you in the middle of her crap from the very beginning. She's done nothing but play on your desire to have a mom." London was trying to comfort me, but it only made me feel like an even bigger idiot.

"How could she look us in the eyes all these weeks, smile, tell us bold-faced lies, then still act like everything was fine? How can someone do that?" I couldn't believe I'd bought it all. Pathetic little girl, that was what I was, needing my mother to kiss the pain away and make everything okay. I was so desperate that I had ignored the signs. I'd ignored them all, wanting to forget everything I knew in my heart. "Why wasn't I happy? Why couldn't I see what was in front of me? I didn't need her. My dad had given us everything. He was the best dad and mom combined." I rubbed my face against the crook of Asher's shoulder as he held me tight against him. "What's wrong with me?"

"Nothing. Nothing is wrong with—"

"I'm just like her, aren't I? The grass is always greener. You said it, that's me. I thought something was better."

"Kitten, we all doubt ourselves at some point. You didn't go off looking for something better, you stayed right where you were. You were more afraid of change than anything else. Don't compare yourself to her. You are so much better, and that is just one of the many reasons I love you."

"Okay. On that, I think we should go." Braden held out a hand to his wife.

"Call me if you need anything." London leaned down and gave Paris a kiss on the top of her head. "Holland, you want to come with us?"

"I was just thinking that." Holland jabbed my shoulder as she walked by. "Bye, Dick," she whispered to Reid as she left, and that one statement somehow broke the solemnity in the room and had us all laughing.

Asher waited until the door closed before lifting me and carrying me to my bedroom. I was dying to be with him. For the last few days, I'd dreamed about kissing Asher and what our real first kiss would feel like. I'd wondered how his body would feel next to mine.

When he finally set me on my feet, I shifted forward, brushing my lips across his and around the edges without actually kissing him. Just light, feathering touches. Every time my bottom lip trailed along his, he stuck out the tip of his tongue, like he needed to taste me.

"Stop teasing me. I want you."

With those three words, *I want you*, I felt my panties dampen and a shiver shoot down my body. My hands were shaking, but I worked them under his T-shirt and lifted it off his sculpted, tanned body. Asher was pure Florida country boy, and I didn't stop the urge to breathe him in and run my tongue along his pecs.

"What are you doing?"

"I want to see if you taste as sweet as you look."

"Do I?"

"No. You're salty." I bit my lower lip.

"You want to lick something salty, well . . ." Asher smirked, obviously figuring out where my mind had gone, and I burst out laughing.

"I love you, Asher Kinkaide, I'm so sorry that it took me a little bit to figure that out. But I'm madly in love with you. I don't know what I'd do without you."

Asher leaned forward and placed a kiss on my left eyelid, then another on my right. "Good thing you'll never have to find out." He lowered his mouth to mine and placed kisses at the corner, slowly working toward the middle. When he reached the point where our lips were aligned, he finally . . . really kissed me. Our lips were coated with want and need. His tongue slid into my mouth and twirled around my own. Every gesture he was making, a foreshadowing of what was to come. Wet and thrusting, our tongues were in a rhythmic dance.

As we continued our kiss, his hands moved to the front of my shirt. He worked on the buttons without breaking our contact and then let it drop to the ground. My bra followed.

Taking one step back, Asher ran his gaze down my body and then back up, taking in every inch of me before bending and bringing my nipple up to his mouth.

The light abrasion from his tongue mixed with the cool air sent goosebumps rippling across my skin. When he stood back up, he moved his fingers to the front of his jeans and unbuttoned them before sliding them off. I watched, hungry to feel every inch of him as he reached for me, unsnapped the stiff denim fabric of my shorts, and then slid his hand into the waistband so he could cup my pussy.

I shivered.

He didn't move at first, which was the sweetest kind of torture, but then ever so slowly, he slid one finger back and forth through the part, coating me with my own juices. "Oh god, Ash, please."

He chuckled and then pulled his hand out so he could free me of the rest of my clothing.

"Let's take a shower," he whispered and then pulled me into the bathroom.

What? No. What was he talking about? The man—who was more god than mortal—was naked with me for the first time ever, and he wanted to shower? I could barely get two brain cells to think about anything other than what he was doing to me, and he was casually turning on the water and stepping under the spray.

Well, I guessed a wet Asher was still okay. Asher's gorgeous, firm body standing under the waterfall was hypnotic. I walked straight to him, and he turned me around, my back to his front, where I could feel his hard erection.

"Relax," he whispered as he trailed one hand lightly down my side, following the curve of my body.

As if it were possible to relax when I was ready to explode.

He knelt down next to me, the water splashing off his muscled back, as he reached for my right ankle, and with his callused fingers, he worked his way up one leg and then back down, only stopping to squirt more of my body wash into his hand and then lathering me up. After sliding one hand up to my breast, he spent several minutes playing with my taut nipples before he moved to my back. Then, adding more soap, he began to massage each arm before working his way around my body, his fingers following suit, and now they were working their way down my spine, and he was spending an inordinate amount of time on each butt cheek before thoroughly washing between my legs. When he reached the front of me, he dropped back to his knees, and I almost fell with him, because I was too turned on to stand. I wanted more, more of him, more of his touches.

"You okay?" The beautiful man was smirking up at me, and I wanted to tell him that I'd never been more okay in my life, but then he was touching me again, and I forgot how to speak.

Back and forth, he cupped water into his hands and washed me before lifting one calf and resting it on his shoulder. Sliding his hands between my legs, he brought them up and behind me to hold me in place, my pussy against his eager mouth.

One lick from his tongue had me almost collapsing again. "Holy shit."

Lick.

When my wet hands slapped against the tiled surface of the shower walls, the sound became the beat for his moves.

Lick.

My hair was soaked and heavy, the long locks slapped against my face as I let my body go to this feeling of ecstasy.

Reaching forward, I shoved my hands into his thick, dark hair, holding his head in that perfectly sweet position. "Oh god, Asher . . ." He pushed his face in deeper, his tongue moving faster as he worked over me, driving me higher and higher until I didn't think I could take it anymore. Then his lips closed around my clit, and the suction was enough to have stars exploding behind my eyes and my whole body erupting with the orgasm.

The sounds from the water, my heart, our breaths . . . they were a symphony.

When he stood, it was several minutes before I was finally able to regain conscious thought. I moved closer to him, turnabout was fair play, after all. "Let's wait until we get out. I need to grab a condom."

Fuck, shit, fuck . . . condom, yes, we need one of those. "I'll get on the pill as soon as possible."

"God, Paris, kill me now."

I smiled, happy to know that he wanted all of me as desperately as I wanted all of him.

ASHER

I turned off the shower, then reached out and grabbed the towels. Wrapping one around her, I let her hold it in place while I quickly dried myself off. Then I turned my whole attention to her. The feel of her body under my hands as I dragged the cloth up and down had me so hard, I was hurting.

"Stay here." I was only gone long enough to grab a condom from my jeans. Racing back to the bathroom, the foil packet in my hands, I started ripping it open.

Paris was desperate for more, reaching to try and take the condom from my hands. "Hurry," she panted. "Make short work of it."

I shook my head at her choice of words and smirked. Quirking one brow, I waited for her words to sink in.

"Oh, I mean long work. Huge work, gigantic work of it. Just get the damn thing on."

Letting out a laugh, I donned the condom, then stepped behind her, sliding my hands down her arms, until I was pressing her hands firmly on either side of the sink.

"Keep these right here," I whispered before sweeping her

149

hair off her shoulder. I dropped slow, open-mouthed kisses along the slope of her shoulder.

"Okay." Her voice was low.

That little breathy sound from her perfect, perfect lips was too much, and yet not nearly enough. I wanted it all. I was still kissing her skin as I slid my hands down her body. My fingers found her heat, then sank deep into the well of her body.

She flexed and then widened her stance a little more, inviting me to take what I wanted. I did, because I needed it all. I needed everything this woman would give me.

Slowly, I rocked them in and out, stretching her and making sure she was nice and ready. I didn't just want her drenched for me. I wanted her begging.

When I couldn't take it anymore and Paris's eyes were the color of dark chocolate, I gripped the base of my cock and guided myself in as I watched her face in the mirror.

The way her lips formed a tight O.

The way her cheeks pulled in as she fought not to scream with ecstasy.

The way her skin turned the shade of a rose as I drove into her again and again.

Me, behind her, us joined, this was us, a team. It was everything I'd ever wanted. We'd always belonged together. I thrust up, and she let out a long moan. I bent slightly and pulled out, then thrust up again, reveling in her cries of pleasure that matched my pace.

"Look at us," I ordered. "I want to"—I shoved up deep —"make love to you"—I pulled back—"for the rest of my life." I pushed up harder.

"Oh god, Asher, please, I'm going to come. Make me come."

"Kitten, you haven't even started to purr yet."

* * *

I COULDN'T BELIEVE how my life had changed as I gazed down at Paris, her head resting on my chest as she watched some chick flick she had seen a hundred times before. It didn't matter how many times she tried to deny it, because if I'd seen it a hundred times, then she had, because there was no way in hell I'd have seen it on my own.

This morning, I had dreaded coming here, and the thought of getting out of my truck and facing her seemed like a distant memory. The hurt from knowing I was going to be in her presence and not be able to touch her had been all for nothing. I looked down at her again and smiled.

I ended up getting everything I'd ever wanted. I looked over at the screen and shook my head. "I don't get it. Why do you always want to watch this movie?" I trailed my fingers through her hair and enjoyed the rhythmic pace of her beating heart.

"I love when Jonah calls in to the radio station and says that his dad needs a wife. Of course, Tom Hanks and Meg Ryan are just perfect. They are very MFEO."

I shook my head. "You're a nut. I don't even know what that means."

"Made For Each Other. It's what that little girl Jessica says about fated love." Paris curled tighter against me. "Kind of like us."

"Yeah, I told you that a long time ago. When are you going to learn to listen?" I was expecting her to say something smartass, but she didn't.

"Will you stay the night with me?"

"I didn't know there was another option. I'm sorry, I finally have you, so there is no way I'm letting you go. But—"

"See . . . there's already a caveat." Paris was trying to be serious, but she was laughing too hard.

"If you will hush for a second, all I was going to say was that I needed to just run home and get a change of clothes." And the ring.

"Oh."

"Yeah, oh." I kissed the top of her head and realized that this was my future, right here.

"Asher, will you start staying here with me? Please. I need you."

"Are you sure? Won't Holland mind?"

"No, she won't, I promise. If it will make you feel better, I'll talk to her, but I know that she won't mind. Hell, she's in the stables all the time anyway."

"Okay, I'll do whatever you want." I kissed the top of her head again.

"Asher?"

"Yes, Kitten?"

"Am I crazy?" I smirked, but she was being serious, so I reined in my sarcasm. "I mean for inviting Cora back into our lives. All she did was cause more of a mess. All I wanted was for it to be like it used to be, when everyone was here for breakfast and we started our day as a family."

"That isn't crazy, that is one of the many things I love about you. And I've missed having our large breakfasts as well."

"Maybe crazy isn't the right word, but naive? I just wanted her to be the mom I remembered, or maybe that I imagined."

"Look at the bright side."

"There's a bright side?"

"There's always a bright side." I buried my face into Paris's long locks and inhaled; she smelled like peaches. She'd been using the same shampoo for as long as I could remember. "If it weren't for you giving Cora a chance, then we never would have gotten around to cleaning out Samuel's room, and that needed to be done."

"Yeah, it really did need to get done."

"See? Bright side. Plus, now you have another part of your dad. Those letters show you a side of him you didn't know. Those yearly photos and how each milestone impacted him." She pushed up from my chest and stared at me. I gripped her chin between my finger and thumb and held her face so she was forced to lock eyes with me. "I love you. I fucking love you."

* * *

EARLY THE NEXT morning before Paris woke, I ran home and got Cujo, my Golden Retriever. I did it more out of guilt than anything else, because he'd been staying at home a lot. I also grabbed some clothes and toiletries before heading back over to the ranch, hoping that I'd be back before Paris woke.

But I should have known.

"Cujo." Paris clapped her hands, and he went running to her. "I've missed you so much." She grabbed a piece of bacon she'd already fried and handed it to him.

"No wonder he loves you more than he loves me."

She clapped her hands together again. "Asher," she said with a smile, holding out a piece of bacon for me.

"Cute. Real cute." I took it anyway. "I figured we could go for a ride later today. What do you think?"

"Sure, whatcha have in mind?"

"I don't know. We just haven't been out on the horses in a while. I'd like to start doing more things together." I tried to think of a nice way to say this without hurting her feeling, but here goes. "Just us, you know?"

"I'd like that. Like date nights. We've always been together, but we haven't really had date nights."

I thought about what Paris had said, but she was wrong: all the things I'd viewed as couple times, she'd viewed as friend time. "You mean like when just you and I go out to dinner? Or when the two of us go to a movie? Or maybe when you want to go for a long ride and we take the top and door off the Jeep and go riding through the woods for hours…just the two of us, then we pull over by the St. John's River and have lunch, stuff like that. Is that what you mean by date stuff?"

Paris tilted her head back and smiled brightly. "You've made your point, smart ass. Okay, so I was a little slow on the uptake."

I lifted one brow.

"Okay, okay. I was real s-l-o-wwwww." Paris dragged out the last word.

"Yeah, that's much more like it."

PARIS

"Who's here?" I moved and peered out the kitchen window. "Crap." At the sound of my exclamation, the rest of my family jumped up to see.

"Cora." Holland shook her head.

"What does that bitch want now?" London asked.

"Want me to handle it?" Braden asked.

"No, Paris needs to," Asher assured them. He knew me so well.

I really did need to handle this. A part of me felt guilty for allowing her back into our lives, so I needed to be the one to push her out. Placing a hand on the doorknob, I waited until I heard her footsteps on the wooden planks of our front porch before pulling it open and meeting her.

"Darling, I've been so worried. I've been trying to call you."

I was stunned that she hadn't felt the icy chill that had swept out of our home, because I sure as hell could feel it.

"Then maybe you should have taken that as a hint," London said from behind me. I turned and slid my hand in front of my throat, signaling for her to stop.

155

"Whatever are you talking about? Why don't you move so we can sit and talk this out?" Cora took a step toward the front door, but then Holland was there, flanking my other side.

"Cora . . ." Cora's eyes widened at my use of her first name, and she stood a little taller. I'd been the one calling her 'Mom' from the get-go. This must have been the first alarm bell that finally penetrated her blasé attitude. "I wanted a mom. I wanted to get to know you, I really did. But more than that, I wanted you to love me, love us." I circled my hand in the air to encompass Holland and London as well. "But the truth is, you love no one but yourself."

"What is going on?" Cora wore a blank expression, as if nothing was penetrating her, or she was truly dumbfounded. But she was smart enough to take one step back.

"We found your letters."

"What letters?" Cora's eyes darted from London to Holland, then back to me.

"Don't play coy. The ones between you and Dad, the ones you obviously thought we'd never see."

"I told you about the letters. Your father returned my letters."

"That is a lie, and you know it. But do you know what I can't figure out? I can't figure out why you were in London's office that day. I know you said that you were dusting, but something about it didn't sit right with me, because you haven't done a single thing since you've been here. You haven't even fixed your own glass of tea, let alone load it into the dishwasher."

"Is that what you were looking for? The letters?" Asher asked from behind me, but Cora didn't answer him. "I have to give you credit, though, you were quick thinking, the way you suddenly fell sick just when Paris got home. I love how you needed her and didn't want to be alone. Yet, you've been without her for almost twenty-two years. Convenient . . . huh?" Asher handed me one of the letters, then wrapped his arms around my waist and pulled me back against his chest.

"Daddy wanted you to come see us, he tried—hell, he even offered to pay for your trip. He sent you money, and nothing penetrated that cold, dead heart of yours. He was so in love with you that he let you treat him like crap." Saying those words hurt me because, for the first time, I wondered if I'd been treating Asher like crap all these years by not acknowledging his feelings. Did he feel like my father had? I promised myself that, no matter how long it took, I would make this up to him.

"Did you know that Dad knew you so well that he figured you'd eventually call Wally? Dad actually told Wally to let you know that he'd passed, he figured that would be the last any of us ever heard from you again," London explained.

"But no, you're like the damn religious door knockers. It doesn't matter what we say to get rid of you, you just keep coming back." Holland smiled, proud of her comment.

But I wanted to get back to Cora and her self-centered ways. "You never cared about him, and you certainly never cared about us. Daddy did a great job, and you know what? I'm glad you left. Imagine having you for a mother. We'd have turned out just as selfish as you are. I thought that I needed a mother, I thought I missed knowing a mother's love, but I didn't, not once. Dad *never* let us feel your absence. Everything I needed to know about how to be a good parent, he taught me. Now, please leave."

She was going to speak again, but Asher stopped her. "Don't, Cora. You've upset Paris enough, and I won't have it."

"You only cared about yourself. We want you gone." London's voice was cold and steady. "I'm glad my daughter won't have one single memory of you. She will only know goodness, and that's from these people inside this house."

"Whatever. Just give me the money that Samuel left me, and I'll be gone."

"What money?" I looked at her, completely aghast. I knew she was cold, but some part of me, small as it was, wanted her to prove me wrong, wanted her to say that she'd learned her lesson and discovered all that she'd been missing.

"I have a letter from him saying he was going to leave me money, plus reimburse me for coming here." Cora's voice was rising. "I won't let you three cheat me out of my money."

"Who are you? You certainly are not the woman I remember." I shook my head as nausea rolled my stomach. She couldn't possibly be serious.

"She's exactly who I remember." London let out a sigh, then she snapped her fingers. "Now I get it. I didn't understand what Daddy meant when he told Wally to relay the message, *tell her she missed her chance.* I bet this was what he was talking about."

"I hate to break it to you, but Dad didn't leave *anything* to you in his will. Maybe he was going to if you came before he died, but we'll never know. The will was read a long time ago, and he left everything to the three of us equally. You weren't named at all in it. You're welcome to call the attorney who handled it, or you can get your own attorney. Just know that you will be spending your own money and getting none in return. You should have enough common sense to know that if you try to sue us for claim on something that you walked away from twenty-two years ago, then we will fight you. By the way, did you ever pay Dad child support for us?" London asked.

Cora's faced turned red.

"Then consider all those years of child support money your inheritance."

"I'd cut my losses if I were you." I stared at the woman in front of me, who was a perfect stranger, and smiled brightly. "If you'd like, we can have the deputy escort you off the property. But you are never welcome here again." I slammed the door and let out a sigh.

Asher tightened his grip. "I know that was hard."

I turned to face him. "No, it really wasn't. After reading those letters, everything just seemed to click into place for me. She really is a stranger, and I feel nothing. Sure, I'd like to have had two parents, who wouldn't? But I didn't miss not having them. My dad was everything." But out of the corner of my eye, I kept Cora in my line of sight, I wasn't trusting her, she'd already proven she couldn't be trusted.

Suddenly I was seven years old again, but this time I wasn't crying, and I didn't feel hopeless or even helpless. No, I felt empowered. I watched Cora's car disappear down the driveway, and a sense of relief washed over me. This was the beginning of a new Paris.

I followed Asher's line of sight and turned to see Marcus, Reid, and Ellie coming up our drive. "What are they doing?"

"I invited them. I hope you don't mind."

"Of course I don't. But what are they carrying?"

"Food. I didn't want you to have to cook, but I wanted us to have a little party."

"What are we celebrating?"

"Us." Asher brought his lips to mine and slowly began to devour my mouth. He only stopped to open the door to welcome everyone.

Holland stepped over and tried to take the food from Reid. "Thanks, I'll take that so you can get back home. I'm sure you have more important stuff to do."

Reid stepped away from her and lifted the food above his head. The man had a good foot in height on her, so there was no hope for her. "Nah, I have it. Plus, there's nothing else I'd rather do than be right here. I always feel so welcome in your home, and now with Asher being here more, I'll probably be around more as well."

"The fuck you will," Holland snapped. "Sorry, Asher, I was rooting for you, but you have to go."

"Don't worry, baby, I'll protect you." I pulled Asher's face down to mine and kissed him again.

"I think I'm going to be sick," Holland hollered from the living room as she stared at us, but she was smiling the whole time she said it.

Marcus had his feet propped up on the coffee table. "Yeah, you two have to put a lid on it or something," he teased.

I stuck my tongue out at Marcus, then at Holland. "You're just jealous that you all don't have anyone to cozy up with. Oh wait . . ." I held up one hand and scanned the room. "We have four extra people without partners. Don't you think it's time that you and Reid stop with all the fighting?" Holland's face turned ten shades of red, a sure sign that I needed to remember to lock my door tonight.

"I just want to officially remind everyone that some murders are worth going to jail for. Braden . . . that's off the record, by the way. Not that I'm ever going to kill my loving sister. Just saying . . . accidents happen." Holland said it coolly and offered a shrug, as though she were the epitome of innocence. The only person who wasn't laughing was Ellie, who obviously wasn't used to Holland's humor.

"Let me get some plates." I took a step to move out of Asher's arms.

"Nope, we have it," Ellie said, reaching into a box and bringing out plates and silverware.

"Ellie, I've been wanting to ask you something." Holland propped one hand on her hip.

"Shoot," Ellie replied.

"How does it feel being an older sibling to an asshole?" I shook my head at Holland, not surprised at all by her quip. Apparently, neither was Ellie.

"Yeah, not answering that. So, Asher really thinks you and I are a lot alike? I just don't see it."

"So you agree, then? That he's an asshole?"

"Sometimes. But sometimes he isn't so bad." Ellie swung out her left foot and kicked Reid. "But I understand why Reid wants me to stay away from you. He must be afraid that I'll either give you ammunition, or that we'll collaborate."

There was silence as everyone waited for Holland's reply. "Hmm. Maybe you have potential, after all."

"Reid, I feel sorry for you." Marcus held up his beer.

"Let's eat." I stepped away and moved toward the table, where London was busy setting everything out. Everyone followed, piling food onto plates and finding seats in the living room.

"This is my favorite part, you know that, right?"

"Eating?" Asher asked quietly.

"No, having everyone together." I was sitting on his lap in Daddy's old recliner. I was so grateful for everyone who was here. "You think there's something going on between your assistant and your brother?"

"Maybe. It would be good for both of them. She's really nice."

"Yeah, she is. I'm sorry that I—" Asher placed his fingertips on my mouth.

"Shhh. It's all good."

When we were done eating, Marcus pulled out several bottles of champagne and uncorked them while Braden set out glasses.

"Are we celebrating Cora being gone?" I scanned the room to see if anyone else was ready to celebrate that as well.

"Nope." Asher turned me in his arms so we were facing each other. "I've asked our friends and family here so we can all be together to celebrate *us*."

"Okay. I'm happy that we're together as well." But I hadn't really thought about a celebration. But that was when I saw it: Asher fumbling in his pocket, then pulling out a Robin's-egg blue box and getting down on one knee.

Oh my god, this was happening. It was so fast. Shit, no, it wasn't. In a way, we've been together for twenty-nine years. Oh my god. Focus, Paris, focus.

"Paris Jean Kelly, there has never been anyone for me but you, from the first time we held hands on the school bus."

I giggled, totally remembering that day. I'd fallen off a horse, and when I landed, I jammed my knee into my mouth, knocking both my front teeth out. I was afraid everyone would make fun of me. "You kept passing me tiny pieces of paper and teaching me how to do spit balls through the gap so I didn't get caught." I chuckled at the memory.

"From the moment you asked me if I'd kiss you because you'd never been kissed, I knew I never wanted to kiss another woman as long as I lived."

"You were afraid that our braces would get caught." I bit my lower lip, because even fifteen years later, I could think about that moment and still feel his lips against my own.

"When you walked down that hall in your prom dress, I knew I'd never see a more beautiful woman in my entire life than you."

I glanced toward the hall he was talking about, the phantom memory right there for me to see.

"But do you know what?"

"What?" I asked, feeling self-conscious.

"All of that pales in comparison to how I felt the moment you finally said you loved me. Will you marry me? Say yes, and that will be the new brightest spot."

"Yes. A thousand times yes." Asher stood and then slid the ring onto the ring finger of my left hand. "Holy shit, I'm engaged."

EPILOGUE

*T*hree months later…

"Holy shit, that man is either going to have a coronary or a boner when he sees you."

"Nice, Holland, real nice. Love how you put those two together." London laughed. "You're stunning, by the way. That dress is perfect for you."

I gazed at my reflection in the cheval mirror that we'd moved into the great room. It was the brightest room in the house, with windows overlooking the back yard and French doors that opened up to the garden area. Plus, we also got the light from the front door and side windows that lined our front porch. With the way the sun was shining, I didn't think I could have chosen a better day.

Today I was going to become Paris Kelly Kinkaide. I'd decided to change my middle name to Kelly, since I never liked Jean anyway. Besides, it was sort of a tradition, since London had done that too.

Yeah, this dress really was perfect. I'd decided to go with the traditional white, but it wasn't a traditional wedding dress. I wanted something with more of that country feel, so my dress was cotton, off the shoulders, and hit mid-calf. But the white tone-on-tone satin plaid ribbon around my waist was my favorite part. My second favorite part was the bouquet. We'd taken a pair of Daddy's boots and had the leather cut into strips, so I could have them woven into the stems of my bouquet. It was my way of having him walk with me down the aisle.

"The back yard is beautiful. Ellie has really done a nice job." London looked out of the back French doors.

I walked to stand next to her. "She really did. I'm glad she turned out to be a good friend. You think she'll find someone?"

"I think she already has." London gave a chin nod in Marcus's direction. He was totally checking her out.

"Would be a great fit. I think she might be able to handle him. It's gonna take a strong woman." I felt sorry for whoever took on that job.

"It will," Holland said as she sidled up to where London and I were standing and I linked my arm around hers.

"Are you sure you want to move? You know that you don't have to, right?" It's the same thing I've said to her every time I've seen her since she told me she was moving out.

"Please, I'm excited. Plus, the last thing I want to hear is, *'Oh god, oh god, oh Asher!'* while I'm trying to get some fucking sleep."

I rolled my eyes. "Get serious."

"I am being serious. You two need some privacy. Besides, it isn't as if I'm moving to a different country. I'm moving into the apartment Dad built above the stables. It's time someone used it. Eventually, I may want to add on or build something bigger, but right now, it's fine for me. This is your home—" Holland waved around the vast area.

"It's your home, too, and London's."

"I know that technically it is, but it's yours as in, you *make* this place a home. I just sleep here. I could sleep anywhere." Holland patted my hand, and I turned to London, who was nodding in agreement. "Don't worry, I still won't buy groceries or cook. I'll eat here."

"Of course you will." I gave my baby sister a squeeze.

"What the fuck is he doing here?" Holland asked, yanking her arm free before racing to the door. The girl was quick in heels and made it to the French doors and flipped the lock just as Reid was walking up the steps. He'd gotten into the same habit of just walking in like everyone else did. When he realized the door wasn't open, he looked up to see Holland in the window, flipping him off.

Sliding around her, I turned the lock and welcomed him. "Come on in."

"Hello to you too, tiger," Reid greeted Holland, but she only growled. "You look beautiful, Paris. Asher is a lucky man."

"Thank you. Is there something you needed?"

"Oh yeah, Braden said to come and get y'all. You ready?"

"Yep. We're ready." I turned around and picked up my bouquet.

And Reid turned and walked back out.

Getting into position, I stood next to London, who was holding Tera in her arms. Holland came and stood on the other side of me. We didn't have a large crowd, just the eight of us, plus Wally and his wife Anne, Jack, another one of our ranch hands, and Mary, Asher's mom. She didn't get out much, but this wasn't something she would miss. I was pretty sure she'd been waiting for this day longer than Asher had. I wasn't overly surprised to discover that she'd had an entire hope chest full of things for me that she'd been collecting over the years. I was shocked, however, to discover she'd been so confident it would be me that the linens were all monogrammed with A.K.P or just an A or P.

With my sisters on either side of me and my eyes locked on the man standing under the trellis next to the minister, I pushed open the French doors and stepped down as Jordan Hill's song played, "Remember Me This Way," from *Casper*. It had been the first movie we'd watched together as kids.

"Look." Holland pointed to a butterfly that had just landed on the bouquet of wild daisies I was holding. "They say butterflies are really angels of our loved ones."

Crooking my head, I took in my baby sister. "That's beautiful, I've never heard you talk like that before."

"Yeah, well, I can be sweet once every ten years or so."

"Do you think Daddy is here? I mean, watching me? He always loved Asher like a son."

"I definitely think he is." Holland squeezed my left arm, and we all watched as the butterfly flittered away.

"Absolutely, he's here." London bumped my shoulder. "Now, it's time for you to put that man out of his misery. He's been waiting a lifetime for you."

I looked to the man in question, and a full-blown grin bloomed on my lips. Apparently, he was done waiting, because he was already halfway down the aisle to me. When he reached my side, he held me close and gazed down at me before he brought one hand up to cup my face, as the other moved to tuck my hair behind my ear. Then he leaned forward and whispered, "Can I keep you?"

That was when I knew this was not just right; it was meant to be. It was the same thing he'd asked me after watching *Casper*, the same line that Casper had asked his cat. And Asher remembered . . . Of course he had, because he was perfect.

"Forever."

Slow Burn Playlist- Paris and Asher

Like I Loved You- Brett Young
Friends in Low Places - Garth Brooks
Shallow- Lady Gaga & Bradley Cooper
How Do I Live - Trisha Yearwood
Remember Me This Way - Jordan Hill
Yours- Russell Dickerson
Meant To Be- Bebe Rexha & Florida Georgia Line
Feels Like Home- Chantal Kreviazuk
Best Day of My Life- American Authors

THANK YOU

- Editing by AW Editing
- Content by Marion Making Manuscripts
- Proofreading by Taryn Lawson
- Proofreading Karen Boston
- L.Woods PR, Veronica Adams
- Personal Assistant Catherine Anderson
- Cover Model, Lori Renee
- Cover Design Russ Norman

MEET DANIELLE

Before becoming a romance writer, Danielle was a body double for Heidi Klum and a backup singer for Adele. Now, she spends her days trying to play keep away from Theo James who won't stop calling her and asking her out.

And all of this happens before she wake up and faces reality where in fact she is a 50 something mom with grown kids, she's been married longer than Theo's been alive, and she now get her kicks riding a Harley.

As far as her body, she thanks, Ben & Jerry's for that as well as gravity. Plus she could never be Adele's backup since she never stops saying the F-word long enough actually to sing.

LETS SOCIALIZE

Website: www.daniellenorman.com
Twitter: @1daniellenorman
Facebook fan page: @authordaniellenorman
Instagram: @1daniellenorman
Amazon Author Page @daniellenorman
Goodreads @daniellenorman
Bookbub: @daniellenorman
Book + Main: @daniellenorman
Official Iron Orchids Reading Group : on facebook
Newsletter: https://bit.ly/DNnews

ALSO BY DANIELLE NORMAN

Iron Orchids Series

Enough- Book 1, Kayson and Ariel

Ebook and Paperback: books2read.com/IronOrchids1

Audiobook: bit.ly/**IronOrchids1**

Almost- Book 2, Carter and Sophie

Ebook and Paperback: books2read.com/IronOrchids2

Audiobook: bit.ly/**IronOrchids2**

Impact- Book 3, Damon and Katy

Ebook and Paperback: books2read.com/IronOrchids3

Audiobook: bit.ly/**IronOrchids3**

Often- Book 4, Ian and Leo

Ebook and Paperback: books2read.com/IronOrchids4

Audiobook: bit.ly/**IronOrchids4**

Until- Book 5, Tristan and Stella, January 2019

books2read.com/IronOrchids5

Iron Horse Series

Stetson- Book 1, London

Ebook and Paperback: books2read.com/IronHorse1

Audiobook: bit.ly/**IronHorse1**, coming November 2018

Slow Burn- Book 2, Paris

Ebook and Paperback: books2read.com/IronHorse2

Audio: Coming Soon

Stallion- Book 3, Holland, coming March 2019

Iron Ladies Series

Getting Even- Book 1, Adeline

Ebook and Paperback: books2read.com/IronLadies1

Available on Audio

Book 2, Sunday, coming soon

Book 3, Olivia, coming soon

Book 4, Melanie, coming soon

ENOUGH

Chapter One
Ariel

MOVING to the happiest fucking place on Earth had nothing to do with fairy tales or finding my Prince Charming. Thanks to my daddy, I no longer believed in magic or happily ever afters. I landed in this city because this was the land of hotels, conventions, and destination weddings, which meant it was my best bet at becoming an event planner.

I didn't hate being a seamstress, but it wasn't my dream, it was my mama's. I never told her that I'd rather be on the other side, planning the events where people wore the fancy clothes, costumes, and uniforms.

I never got the chance.

During my freshman year of high school, she had her first stroke, spoke with a slur, and relied a little more on me. But just before my senior year, Mama had her second stroke, and someone needed to keep the business going to pay the bills, so I took over. Because Daddy was long gone, he had no use for an invalid wife, and no interest in raising a teenage daughter who hated him.

I told myself repeatedly that Mama would have wanted me to follow my dream, even if it meant hers was gone. Though, I doubted that included buying a motorcycle.

I BRUSHED the wetness away then strapped on my helmet and headed to my motorcycle. Ever since binge watching *Sons of Anarchy*, I wanted to be badass. Okay, not like crime badass. Just the I-look-cool-on-this-bike kind of badass. So, after I unpacked my last box, I went out and purchased a Harley Sportster. I couldn't wait to start the engine and let the wind whip across my face. It was cathartic. As the engine roared to life, I replayed the words my teacher said just a few weeks ago during motorcycle safety class.

Ease up on the throttle.

Hold steady.

Don't freak.

The bike will go where your eyes go.

I found myself twisting the throttle a little more than I should have, and a small smile pulled at my lips.

I shifted gears and headed to the service road around the Mall at Millennia, Orlando's version of Rodeo Drive. Since I lived in metro Orlando, finding somewhere to practice riding wasn't easy. There were always constant road improvements or tourists who drove like idiots reversing down the interstate because they missed the fucking exit. So, the rarely traversed area behind the mall was one of the best places to practice.

It was also one of the only places I'd practiced. I stayed within a five-mile radius of my home, but I needed to get comfortable and feel confident so I could take my bike out for a long ride, let the sun shine down on my face and forget the reality that was my life.

After a few laps around the mall, I pulled my bike into a parking spot, headed inside to grab a drink, and was walking back out to my bike when two men dressed all in black cut between two cars.

They reminded me of Crabbe and Goyle from the Harry Potter movies, and I was still watching them from the corner of my eye when they broke into a run. There was nothing oaf-like or klutzy about them. Maybe they had just robbed Tiffany's or Cartier? That didn't seem right, though. There were no security guards chasing them. No alarms going off or police cruisers peeling into the lot.

Eyebrows dipping, I paused. Watching.

The two men zigzagged through another section of cars, and the one on the left pointed in my direction. In that earth-shattering moment it connected—they were after me. I ran. Fuck. I had no clue what to do. I would never be able to start my bike and get away quick enough. Their footsteps got closer then stopped. I turned around just as the two men separated, one going left the other going right, moving in an arc around me. They were corralling me like a caged animal.

"Help!" I shouted just before a hand clamped over my mouth.

"Shut the fuck up, bitch," a husky voice commanded. I

didn't. I continued to try to scream as I kicked and hit him. Biting. I raked my nails down his forearm, his face, his shoulder—wherever I could dig my nails. I wasn't going with these men willingly.

People say your life flashes before your eyes in times of crisis, when what they mean is that you replay your life in slow motion.

In those brief moments, it seemed as if I relived that day when everything seemed to unravel.

Mama sitting at her sewing table as she looked up and hollered, "Close that door. You weren't born in a barn."

And I'd had it, she kept forgiving him. "Why do you stay married to him? All day long Billie Sue Werner ran around school telling the entire freshman class that her mama saw Daddy parked by the railroad tracks with Ms. Kinney, and they were 'going at it.' It's the same thing Daddy does almost every night just with different women. You know it, I know it, the whole town knows it, Mama. And they're laughing at us."

I marched back through the house and slammed the door shut. This was just one of the many things I hated about living in a small town, everybody knew your business, and nothing ever changed.

"You go get your homework done, you hear me?"

"Yes, I hear you. But do you hear me? Mama, I'm serious. I'm leaving. I can take no more."

That was when Mama's face took on an ashen appearance and she collapsed.

I learned real fast how wrong I was, I could take more. In fact, it was shoved down my throat, heaped on my shoulders, and I was still taking it.

The brief flash from my past was shattered by the smell of days-old sweat on the man holding me. My body revolted, my mouth went watery, and my stomach lurched with the sour taste curdling on my tongue. I was going to vomit, and there was nothing I could do to stop it.

"Fucking watch it, man. We ain't supposed to hurt her, just scare her." The guy I nicknamed Crabbe had a Hispanic accent and seemed a bit uncomfortable about what they were doing.

I broke free from the Goyle-dude as he argued back.

Scare me? Scare me? What the fuck? "Help!" My shout rang out across the parking lot. "Fine. You scared me. Let me go!"

They came at me again, obviously not convinced that I was scared enough. They circled me, Crabbe in front and Goyle-dude at my back. The guy behind me wrapped his arms around my chest, restraining me and lifted me off the ground. The toes of my left shoe scraped the concrete, giving me just enough leverage to pull my leg back and aim for the fat guy's nuts.

"Help!" I shouted again and again until my throat burned

Someone had to hear me. There had to be someone! I refused to cry, not yet, not there, I needed to get a grip on at least one of these men. Anything. Anywhere. These bastards, whoever they were, were not going to get away with what they were trying to do. I had to break free long enough to pull off their damn masks, at least one of their masks. If I survived, I wanted to be able to identify these sons of bitches. I didn't get the chance, though.

Untrimmed nails bit into my ankles as the other thug grabbed my legs.

"Let's go," Goyle-dude ordered.

I bucked, twisted, and tried to get away as they carried me like a piece of furniture.

Then I heard it, a shout in the distance.

"Police! Freeze!"

In their haste to escape, the men dropped me, I scrambled to right myself and get my feet under me. My head snapped back, pain shot through my scalp as one of the men grabbed a fistful of my hair and slammed me forward. My face met the hood of a car with a sickening *crack*. The wet heat of my own blood and searing pain were the only things I registered before the man yanked back one more time. I didn't have time to put my hands up as my face barreled toward a window and I hit the car again, this time with enough force to knock me out.

I awoke on the ground, the burning hot pavement seared through my skin and deep down to my bones. Tiny pieces of gravel and sand pressed into my skin. I wasn't sure how long I'd been lying there, but I was hyperaware and could feel every single pebble and grain.

Gentle fingers wrapped around my wrist that rested at my side. I felt the brush of a watchband against my palm and scratch of calluses over my skin. Somehow, I was alert enough to process that this was a man's hand. He pressed two fingers to the underside of my wrist. It took a few more seconds to realize that he was checking for a pulse, and then the fear set in that my attackers were back.

I tried to get up, but I couldn't move, I ached too badly.

"Help," I begged, but my voice sounded like a gurgle, a sound that even I didn't recognize escaping my lips.

Lights flashed around me. I didn't understand where all the lights were coming from. My mind too clouded with fear, it took me several seconds to realize that they were prisms dancing in tiny shards of glass that surrounded me.

The hand on my wrist was gone, and a moment later, a man's face came into my field of vision.

"Can you hear me? I am Deputy Kayson Christakos; I'm

here to rescue you. Paramedics are on the way. Don't try to move. You're safe."

Blink.

Our eyes locked.

Blink.

I saw stars. No . . . a star. Then I passed out, again.

STETSON

Chapter One
London

WHY WERE funeral home's chairs so uncomfortable? Did they have a catalog of nothing but hardwood, straight-back chairs? Chairs that constantly reminded you that you were uncomfortable, the people around you were uncomfortable, and that you were going to be uncomfortable for another two hours.

Maybe they did it so that you wouldn't be distracted from the people walking by and reminding you of how fabulous your father was or how every day since you learned about his lung cancer that you worried. Nope, they wouldn't want you to miss a second of being reminded of how worried you were about not being able to fill his shoes.

Worried that you would let your sisters down.

Worried that despite everything—despite your father having raised you to believe that girls were just as great as boys—maybe the farm might have been better off in the hands of a son. That was if Samuel Kelly had had a son, but he didn't. He'd been stuck with three daughters and a wife that had run off when the girls were little.

"I'm sorry for your loss." I was pulled from my thoughts and self-doubt to accept more condolences.

"Your family is in our prayers."

"Let us know if you girls need anything."

"Your father was a good man."

Were condolences like straws and everyone drew one; whatever was written on the straw was the platitude you had to repeat?

I looked at my sisters to make sure that they were holding up. Part of me felt relieved because I knew that Daddy wasn't in pain anymore, but at the same time, I was pissed at him for leaving us. It didn't matter that I was thirty—nothing made you feel like you were a little girl all over again than losing a parent.

The pastor finished the service, and my sisters and I followed the pallbearers, who carried my father's casket out the doors of the church.

Sweat trickled down my back, and I found myself more focused on the riding lawn mower I could see in the distance than I was on what was being said as they lowered Daddy's casket into the ground. Taking a deep breath, I inhaled the scent of fresh mowed grass and impending rain. It was going to rain, I could smell the saltiness in the air, and when I opened my mouth I could taste the saltiness on the tip of my tongue.

Who was I kidding? It always rained in Florida, especially this time of the year, and the rain was always salty thanks to being close to the ocean. But right then I needed the rain, I begged for it. I wanted it to pour and send all these people scurrying for cover so that I could sit here for a few moments and say goodbye to my hero.

I was on autopilot, my focus was up toward the horizon and the rain rolling in, while people were kissing my cheek, saying goodbye, and then walking off. Person after person stopped, but I was moving out of natural reaction.

"You okay, London?" I looked at my sister Paris as she tucked a few loose strands of hair behind my ear. "You seem like you're a million miles away."

"I'm fine, just tired. Let's go home." I stood and held out one hand for each of my sisters. Being the oldest, I'd always felt a heavy amount of responsibility for them, and right then, I needed not to be the weak one.

The three of us headed to my truck. Jumping up into the seat, I paused for a second before pulling my legs in to kick off any excess dirt that still clung to my heels. Nothing about Geneva was fancy, not even the cemetery, where I had to walk through, dirt, sand, and stand in soft sod while I watched my father be lowered into the ground. After removing my hat—because in our little town you always wore a black hat to a funeral—I laid it on the console and started the engine. As I glanced into my rearview mirror, I met the eyes of my baby sister Holland, who hadn't said a word, which was so strange since of the three of us, she was always the most outspoken one.

But I wanted to get this day over with, which was probably why we had bucked tradition and decided not to have a potluck after the funeral. People from the church had been bringing food by for the last month while Daddy was in hospice. I just didn't want any more people traipsing in and out of the house telling us how sorry they were, which in the end ultimately led them to discussing the fact that none of us were married and someone was bound to offer up one of their relatives to help us out. As if we were so desperate to find a husband that we needed someone to give us their cousin's son, who was probably still living in his mom's basement and went by the name of Bubba. No thanks.

I drove the five miles to our home, the one that I grew up in, the one that still smelled of oiled leather. The smell was an ever-present reminder of when Dad would bring the saddles in and sit there with a polishing cloth, and I realized that I wasn't ready to go in, not yet.

"You coming?" Holland stood in the doorway, front door ajar, waiting for me.

"Hey, I'll be back later. I'm going up to Marcus's."

Or, more specifically, the Elbow Room, which was the bar he owned. Holland nodded, and I was back in my truck before the door even closed behind her.

Fifteen minutes later, I was pulling open the door and walking into the dimly lit space that smelled of old smoke. It had been a few years since people were allowed to smoke inside, but the scent that was imbedded into the structure assuaged me. That smell wasn't ever leaving. I remember when the previous owner had the place and my daddy would bring me up here as a kid, there were nights that the smoke had been so thick you could practically cut it with a knife. There had been no hope for the air filtration system to keep up.

I waved at Marcus, who had already changed out of his dark suit and was wearing a T-shirt with the bar's logo on the back, and slid into an empty stool. He and his brother had been two of Daddy's pallbearers, but you wouldn't have known it if you hadn't been there. He looked as if today was just another day.

"Well, I do believe I have my passport ready," he hollered. I knew that he was trying to lift my spirits.

"You may see London and you may see France, but you'll never see my underpants." I retorted, and I caught the beer he slid me down the well-worn pine top bar.

I was used to all the comments and jokes about my name, had to be. When you were raised with two sisters and you all had names of fancy destinations, people expected you to be well...fancy. They were always shocked to realize that the only thing fancy about the Kelly girls were their names. The fancy one had been our mama, which was why she ran off with the first guy who promised to show her the world when I was ten years old. She'd wanted more than farm life. But not me, I could spend my days running the fields on Madam Mim, my horse.

I downed my first beer, slammed the bottle onto the counter a bit too hard, and smiled when I realized that Marcus had been anticipating my mood and had the second one waiting. I started drinking as I scanned the room. The place was a cross between a dive bar and a honky-tonk. The walls were crowded with memorabilia from locals who had made it big or famous people who had visited. There were several photos from the movie *The Waterboy* with Adam Sandler since the bonfire party was actually filmed right here in Geneva, Florida. They also filmed a few episodes of *ER* with George Clooney here. That was when I was young and boys were still yucky, but I remembered all the moms and teachers going crazy.

M.J. Tucker, a guy I went to high school with, was sitting at one of the corner booths, and I shook my head. I seriously considered calling his wife since he was hitting on Etta Hill. She knew—hell, everyone knew that M.J. was married. Then again, we also knew that Etta's last name suited her perfectly, she was still the easiest hill to climb. Some things never changed, no matter how long it had been since high school.

"Another one, please." I turned to face Marcus to make sure that he'd heard me. He was standing behind the counter, lost in space.

I took a long swig, I hadn't realized how thirsty I'd been, two beers in ten minutes was fast even for me. Shaking my head at my realization, I followed the direction of Marcus's gaze and saw a couple of women wearing denim miniskirts and crop tops. I fought back my urge to laugh at their shiny new cowboy boots. They were wannabes. Wannabe cowgirls, wannabe older than they were, and wannabe someone's one-night stand.

Rolling my eyes, I waved a hand in front of Marcus's face to get his attention. The man always lost his shit around booty and breasts. Once again, some things never changed.

I cleared my throat and waited with a giant grin on my face.

"Holy shit, London, you just got here. You might want to slow down a bit." He cleared away the bottle but still reached behind him and grabbed me another.

"Don't judge, you know damn well that it's been a hard day."

"But you're driving." Marcus tried to argue before handing me the bottle. "Just promise me that you aren't leaving until I say so."

I chuckled dryly and nodded. Yeah, I had no intention of wrapping myself around some telephone pole.

"How you holding up?"

"Really? I'm in a bar, dressed all in black, and resembling a lost little girl. Worse yet, I feel like one. Can we talk about something else, anything?" I took a swig from the bottle and wiped my mouth with the back of my hand. Not the most ladylike action, but it was fitting for the way I was feeling.

"Have you checked out the latest *Hustler* magazine?"

"Holy shit, Marcus." I laughed so hard I almost choked on my drink. "Don't tell me you read that shit. Oh my god, I don't know that I've ever seen one."

"That's my girl, that's the laugh I've been missing." Marcus reached forward and wrapped his giant paw of a hand around mine.

"You know you wouldn't have to resort to those types of magazines if you'd stop being such a commitment-phobe. I swear that I don't know who is more sex depraved, you or the women you hook up with."

I'd been ragging on him since high school when our world was divided into two groups: helmet head or fans of helmet heads. And group two was what the helmet heads called Future Fags of America, otherwise known as FFA. Marcus and I were FFA all because we grew up on farms. But both groups had their own set of popular kids, except for Marcus, he was the one that was determined to buck the system. He wanted to sample the goods on both sides of the fence.

"Look who's talking. When was your last relationship? Oh wait, never because you are too damn committed to the ranch. You need to get out and have some fun, let loose. We need to go out sometime—you can be my wingman and help me find someone and I'll help you."

"God, I love you, Marcus, but the last thing I want to do is let you loose on my own species. You are what I like to call a man whore."

Trying to feign injury, he threw his hands over his heart and acted as if my words were causing him to have a heart attack.

"You know that does not work on me, right?"

"If you disapprove of my love life so much, then maybe you should be my dating coach, tell me what I'm doing wrong and how to find, you know, the one."

Whoosh, my beer spewed everywhere. "Fuck, warn a girl next time you're going to say something like that, won't you?"

"Is someone choking? I know mouth-to-mouth. Hey, Marcus, a bottle of beer, please."

I turned at the familiar baritone voice and tried to ignore the way it sent shivers straight to all the right parts of me. I slowly moved my eyes from his boots up his jeans, to his black T-shirt, and then to the gorgeous face. Yep, speaking of man whore, it was Braden Fucking McManus.

"You okay there, London? I'm assuming that you really don't need mouth-to-mouth."

"That's debatable, depends who's asking. If you're offering." I threw my hands over my mouth. Oh shit, I said that aloud. It was supposed to stay in my head. Beer, I had beer tongue. That slippery thing that held nothing in.

Braden coughed, making me think that maybe he was the one that needed the mouth-to-mouth and I'd be willing to practice on him.

Embracing my alcohol-infused bravado, I dropped my hand and gave him a wink instead of cowering away from my slip-up.

"You'll have to excuse her, Deputy, she's had a bit much tonight." Marcus laughed as he looked at me and tried to extract the bottle from my hands, but I held on for dear life.

"Shut up, this is only my third," I mumbled to Marcus even though he wasn't paying attention. Oh my God, this was Braden fucking McManus. I'd had a crush on him since we were in middle school. Of course, we never spoke because he was too busy being homecoming king, prom king, and the class president. He'd always been so out of my league.

I averted my gaze from Marcus and turned toward Braden. His muscled arms flexing was almost as good as watching porn. I could totally get off to this. Damn. The protruding veins made it difficult not to look at him.

Braden moved his arm to take a swig off his bottle, and it finally broke my hypnotic lock on him. I glanced up and noticed that he'd been watching me.

I gave him a head bob.

What?

I gave him a fucking head bob. The only thing missing was the Jersey accent, and I would have been all Joey Tribbiani from friends. "How you doin'?" I wasn't cool. I couldn't pull that off. What was I saying? Even Joey Tribbiani couldn't pull that off.

"So, Sergeant, what are you doing in here tonight?" Marcus continued talking as if I hadn't just made a fool of myself. I owed the guy a home cooked meal. Thank you, Marcus.

"I'm a lieutenant now. But Braden is fine. I just got assigned back to the East District, so I thought I'd pop in."

The two chatted about Braden being back in Geneva, and I sat there listening. God, even his neck was sexy.

Braden cut his attention to me. "How you doing, London? I heard about your dad. I'm sorry for your loss."

I nodded my thanks and took another swig of my beer.

"Is it true that you're going to stay and run the ranch?"

"Mm-hmm." Voice, London, use your voice, I mentally reprimanded myself. "Yeah, my sisters and I. We each have our own skills anyway. I've always handled the books and the cattle ranch, Holland is a horse whisperer if there ever was one, and Paris is a whiz with organic stuff. She keeps our fields beautiful so the horses and cattle always have new grazing areas. Between the three of us, we might equal one Samuel Kelly."

"I'm sure you'll make your dad proud."

Marcus smirked playfully as he stole glances at me, trying to tear me from my melancholy and tease me because he knew that I'd had a crush on Braden McManus since we were in sixth grade. I swallowed the lump that formed in my throat and shot Marcus a deadly glare. Braden looked at me, then nodded lightly. He had this presence about him, and it was overwhelming.

Or at least I was overwhelmed when he slid onto the barstool next to me and made himself comfortable as if he was going to stay a while. The air around me got thin, making it hard to breathe.

I studied his face a bit longer in the dim lighting of the club. He was absolutely one of those men who only got better looking with age. He was rugged with his steel jaw, which seemed to have been carved by an expert sculptor and gave him a calculated edginess. His hair was almost black and was messy in a way that could have been an accident or could have taken him fifteen minutes to get it to look like that. His mouth...oh, that mouth, it was curled into a friendly, inviting grin.

I'd bend over backward for my sisters, but Braden McManus, I'd bend over forward for.

Damn it, London, don't go there.

The trance I was in was broken when I heard Marcus faking a cough. Out of the corner of my eyes, I saw his mouth crack in to a mischievous grin. "So, Braden, how's the family?" Marcus asked as he grabbed a cloth and wiped off the bar.

"Good, Mom and Dad still live in the same house. I think that my mom is enjoying being retired, but my dad is bored as hell."

"How about your wife?" Marcus held up one finger. "Hold that thought." Marcus turned to answer the phone, which left me with nothing to do but wonder who the hell Braden had married. Was he happy? I bet she was beautiful. He probably married some cheerleader type.

"Hey, I gotta run, that was my mom." Marcus lifted the half-door that kept people from walking behind the bar.

"Is everything okay?" I leaned forward on my elbows, and my heart ached with worry for Marcus and his brother, Asher. Marcus's mom was several years older than my dad had been, and something happening to her today of all days was almost too much.

"Yeah, she's fine, but I have to run. Don't worry about your tab; they're on me. If you need anything else, just ask Jett." He gestured toward the bartender at the other end of the bar before adding, "Braden, it was nice seeing you, and I hope you stop in again."

"I'll start coming by more." Braden held out his hand, and the men shook before Marcus turned to me. "Listen to me, call your sisters or call my brother, hear me?"

"Don't worry about it, I'll make sure she's fine," Braden assured him.

I rolled my eyes and then gave Marcus my most motherly stare. "I better not find out that you skipped out for some booty call. You know that it's okay to have a dick with standards."

I turned my gaze to Braden, who was beating his chest and making a loud choking noise. "You okay there?" I patted his back and felt his body heat radiate through my fingers.

"Yep, I might be the one who needs mouth-to-mouth. I just never imagined hearing London Kelly saying something like that. The girl I remember was much quieter."

Marcus let out a loud snort. "Amazing how girls can fool you, huh?"

I shook my head, trying to clear away the thoughts of putting my mouth to Braden's mouth, and decided that one more beer shouldn't hurt, four wasn't going to kill me, it would just help get rid of that thing...shit...what was it called? Oh yeah, a filter. "Jett, can you hand me another beer?"

GETTING EVEN

Chapter One
Adeline

THE SCREECHING SOUND of the tires as the V8 American muscle car pulled into a parking space in one fell swoop was one of Adeline Morgan's favorite sounds in the world. The only thing better than that was shopping.

She sat in her seat a few minutes and let the song, which was playing far too loudly, finish before she cut the engine. The abrupt absence of the rumble and music in the afternoon air hit Adeline like a shiver of anxiety. There was a comfort in all things car and speed, but she was late, so she forced herself not to crank the engine again.

Adeline pushed the solid steel door open and slid from her seat before straightening her black bodycon dress, which clung on to her curvy figure. Then she slipped her four-inch black leather heels back on—one did not drive a muscle car with heels on—and grabbed the bags from the passenger seat.

The Iron Ladies office took up the majority of the fourth floor of one of the many tall buildings in downtown Orlando, and it was more of a home to her than her actual house was. The main office, like other rooms in the company, stood immaculate with white walls and floor-to-ceiling windows that revealed a large view of the city.

Adeline walked past the desks that sat in an open floor plan and into the boardroom. A large oil painting of giant handcuffs hung on the opposite wall, and in the center of the room was a large mahogany table. Around said table were some unhappy faces. Well, all except Melanie, she was pacing the room.

"Where the fuck have you been?" Melanie stopped pacing long enough to glare at Adeline. "Really? The client's been waiting nearly an hour."

Adeline shrugged and fell into her seat next to Sunday before setting her bags onto the table in front of her. "Sorry, my lunch break lasted longer than usual."

"Told you so," Sunday said a little too happy.

Adeline winked at Sunday. "No one knows me better than you do."

"Depends what truck stop we go to, I'm sure there's a few bathroom's that have poetry written in your honor and we could learn a thing or two." Olivia reached into her pocket, pulled out some money, and handed it over to Sunday, obviously having lost a bet. Sunday grinned triumphantly, tossed Adeline half the take, and turned back to her laptop.

Adeline flipped Olivia off and laughed, knowing full well that Olivia's harsh barb was only a joke.

"Well, now that we're finally all here, can we interview the client already?" Melanie asked, glaring between the two of them.

"Fine by me," Sunday said, clearly not really paying attention she was too absorbed in her computer.

"Who's the client anyway?" Adeline asked.

"Some lady." Sunday never lifted her eyes from her laptop screen.

Adeline rolled her eyes. "You think? I was assuming that we were still Iron Ladies and not men. But, then again, maybe you all voted to change that while I was out."

Olivia sighed. "How about I bring her in for the interview, and thereafter you two can argue about whatever gender you think the client is?"

"Whoa, someone's in a bad mood today." Adeline let out a low whistle.

"Adeline, you're late . . . again. You come in here with this I-don't-care attitude. But, damn it, I know you well enough to know that, if I look in those bags, there is probably something for me in there that I'm going to love." Olivia slapped her hands onto the table as Adeline leaned forward, reached into the aforementioned bags, and pulled out the most awesome black leather vest.

"I'll get her." Melanie headed toward the boardroom doors. "And for goodness' sake, Olivia. Put that thing away."

"Yeah, Olivia, put that thing away." Adeline smiled as Olivia gathered her oil rag and kit to start reassembling her baby Glock.

One of their founding and non-negotiable rules was that all four members had to be present for the first meet with all potential clients. The rule had been Melanie's idea, and according to her, it presented a professional and united front to the client. Melanie had also stressed the importance of making a good first impression to the client, which was another important reason for all members to be present for first contact. Finally, all four members had to state their opinion and cast their vote on whether they should take the case. Majority always won. The rules may sound stupid, but it was these cornerstones that had made the Iron ladies an underground success. Oh, to most, they were just everyday businesswomen, but to the women who were passed the orchid-colored card, they were more than that.

When Melanie returned with their client, Adeline let out a muted groan. It was Loren fucking Delaney. She was every-thing that Adeline knew her to be—cultured, elegant, collected, classy, and the fucking mayor of Orlando's wife.

"We apologize for the delay, Mrs. Delaney." Melanie ushered Loren to a seat at the head of the table. Melanie, Sunday, and Olivia cast glances at Adeline. "I don't suppose you've met our fourth member Adeline yet?"

"Hello, Adeline, it's nice to meet you. Thank you all for agreeing to meet me." Loren gave a wave to Adeline.

"Do you have something for us?" Adeline asked.

"Oh, yes, I do." Loren reached into her purse and pulled out the secret orchid colored business card, it was the only proof that the Iron Ladies existed. They didn't advertise, they weren't listed in a phonebook, nor did they have a website. They operated simply by referrals.

Melanie took the card. "So, Mrs. Delaney—"

"Please, call me Loren."

"Okay," Melanie continued. "Loren, since you contacted us, I take it that you were given our card by one of your friends."

"Yes, by—"

Melanie held up one hand to stop Loren from continuing. "Please, we keep everyone's privacy."

Loren nodded her understanding.

"Then you also understand that this meeting is an interview and not a guarantee that we will take your case?"

Loren folded her hands in her lap, but Adeline paid close attention to the slight shake of her shoulders.

"You are aware that we are not your normal private investigator service? As such, our fees reflect our exceptional services."

Again, Loren nodded. "I really do hope that you take my case, though."

Sunday looked away from her computer and met Loren's eyes. "As you're aware, one of our services includes helping women whose husbands are . . . assholes?" Loren suppressed a laugh. "Since you're here, I'm assuming that the mayor has been very, ummm, assholey?"

"To say the least," Loren concurred.

"We need you to tell us why you are here." Melanie shot Adeline a glare for not waiting her turn.

"Please excuse my colleague," Melanie snapped. "We aren't trying to rush you."

"Well, . . . actually, I kinda am," Adeline quipped.

"Adeline." Melanie gritted her teeth.

"He's the fucking mayor, that spells trouble." A big part of the Iron Ladies success was dependent on staying below the radar, and there was nothing above the radar more than a fucking politician.

Olivia interrupted, "I think most of the talking needs to come from Loren."

"Agreed." Melanie nodded.

Loren looked down at her hands as if she was contemplating each word. "I met Greg when I was an intern at his law office. I like to think I was actually on my way to being a talented lawyer, but when Greg made me an offer to work alongside him in his organization, I took it without hesitation." Loren paused to study the faces of her audience.

"Go on, Loren," Adeline encouraged her.

"So, I worked for him as an intern. At first, I was intimidated by him since he had such temper. You know, one moment calm and the next, there were papers and objects flying across the room. He got stirred up by the littlest things. He hid it well, and only those closest to him ever saw it. Everyone else thought he was perfect. I knew he had goals to run for office, so I overlooked a lot because I knew it would be great for my career." Loren laughed, but it was a watery sound that had Olivia passing over the box of tissues they kept in the room for just that reason.

"Thank you." Loren wiped her tears and forced a tight smile. "I'm fine. Anyway . . ." She pulled in a calming breath. "We started dating a few months after I took the job, and a year later, we were married. I genuinely thought that he had loved me, but all he really loved was what I did for his image. It took me five years to figure out that the only reason he married me was because he needed a wife who fit the ideal image for his political aspirations." Loren played with the tissue in her hands, and slowly shredded it without realizing her actions. "Our marriage, it isn't real, nothing about it is real. We never talk, well, not unless we are in public, then he seems interested in me. He's a good actor . . ." Loren let out a chuckle. "Even I was fooled. Occasionally, we had sex . . . plain old vanilla, emotionless sex. But that isn't even once a month. We all know that if he isn't getting it at home, he's getting it somewhere. Every time I try to ask him about it or even ask him if he's coming home, he goes off on me. We are probably up to World War eighteen thousand in our house. Everything turns into a war."

Adeline leaned forward and gave Loren's arm a reassuring squeeze.

"The thing is, I'm tired of the pretense, of the coldness. I want a real marriage, not just something that appears perfect from the outside. I want to be happy. I want my daughter to be happy. I've endured all this time because of my little girl, and I've realized that she shouldn't be in a loveless family. I want to teach her that she deserves to be loved."

"Have you called an attorney? Why not just file for a divorce?"

Loren grabbed another tissue and played with it like a worry stone. "No, I haven't because as soon as he catches wind of this, I won't be able to fight him. If there is anything in this world Greg cherishes, it's his reputation, and guys like Greg don't allow their wives to leave them. It's as much about control as it is anything else."

This was always Adeline's least favorite part of the interview process, not because she hated meeting new clients but because this was when it felt like pulling teeth just to get a straight answer. Nothing was short and to the point.

"Do you think that Greg would try and hurt you if he found out?"

"Not physically hurt me but I need you to know that Greg is up for reelection and he has aspirations for governor someday. He views appearances as a vital part to his image. His career comes before anybody else. He can be ruthless, and when this all blows over, he isn't going to spare me. If I don't have enough to evidence against him then he will use his clout to make the courts view me as a bad mother. He doesn't want custody of Noelle, our daughter, but he'll do it just to hurt me and try to control me. Noelle is scared of him, she hides from him because he screams all the time. I desperately need your help."

Something in Adeline's gut was telling her that this case

was a hard no, it was spelling trouble. "What do you think we might be able to find about Greg, what kind of evidence?"

"My grandparents owned a lot of property around central Florida and they left me a parcel of about five-thousand acres as part of my trust. It has been valued at about five million dollars and is prime real estate. Just before Greg and I got married, I had an attorney set it up for a trust for our first child. Once Noelle was born, I had her name put on the property. I asked Greg about it a few months ago because I didn't get a tax bill in this year. It always comes in my name as the custodian for Noelle. He said that he'd look into it, but when I asked about it again he got mad at me. So, I went to the property appraiser's page and looked up the information, but the info was hidden."

"Hidden?"

"Yeah, hidden. You can file to have your property address hidden on all tax records and driver's license if you are law enforcement or in a government position. It keeps people from looking you up and then showing up at your house. Our home address is hidden, but I couldn't have the land done since it was under my maiden name and Noelle's name."

"So, what are you suggesting?"

"I'm not entirely sure. I just know that something isn't right about the situation, and no one at the property appraiser's office will release any information to me."

"But, you're the owner of the property, right? Why wouldn't they talk to you about it?"

"I don't know. All I know is that when I couldn't find anything online, I called them, and the man who answered told me that he couldn't give me any information because of the Privacy Act. I tried to explain to him that he didn't need to protect my own privacy from me, but he apologized again and hung up."

"And you think that Greg has done something behind your back?" Adeline asked.

"Yes. In fact, I'm almost positive because I overheard a conversation that he had with someone. He was on the phone one night and I heard him talking about the land. That was the night before I called you. He's the mayor, if he catches on to any of this he will discredit me, so before I do anything, I need proof that he's having an affair for the prenuptial. I need proof of his temper to keep him from taking my daughter, and I need to find out what he did with my inheritance. He is underhanded. I don't want him to be able to turn people against me and blame it on me just being a bitter woman. I want undeniable proof that he's a cheating-underhanded-asshole."

Olivia, Sunday, Adeline, and Melanie were silent for a second, waiting to see if Loren had any other bombs to drop. When the woman just continued to fidget, Melanie smiled and stood.

"Thank you, Loren, you've given us a lot to consider. We need to discuss what you've told us and do a little research on our own before we can give you our answer. We, of course, will try to get back to you as soon as possible and will keep you posted about our next meeting with you." Melanie shook Loren's hand across the table. Adeline, Sunday, and Olivia followed suit, each extending a hand one at a time to Loren.

"It was nice having this opportunity with all of you. I really hope you consider this . . . if not for me, for my daughter."

Melanie held the boardroom doors open and escorted Loren out. When the doors shut, Adeline, Sunday, and Olivia sighed in unison.

"Holy fucking shit. Loren Delaney, who would have thought?" Adeline shook her head, not believing what she had just witnessed. "On television and in the newspapers, they come across as being a happy couple. Just goes to show you that there's no such thing as a perfect marriage. What's this world coming to when women that look like fucking June Cleaver can't keep a man? I can see the tagline now, don't take it so hard Beaver."

Olivia turned to stare at Adeline, her mouth agape. "I have no fucking clue where you come up with this shit."

Adeline shrugged her shoulders. "It's a gift, what can I say."

Melanie shook her head. "Well, let's get back to business, you know the drill." She arched one eyebrow and locked eyes with Adeline. "What do you think? It seems like you're against us helping her, Adeline." Melanie made a few notes in her notebook.

"Trouble. Politicians are all trouble. He's going to have every city office coming down on us. We are going to lose our business license and the fire marshal is suddenly going to find fifty things to fine us over before shutting us down."

"I think she needs our help and we can give it," Olivia explained.

"Don't they all?" Adeline asked.

Sunday peered over her laptop. "I liked her."

Adeline gave her a deadpan look. "I'd like to meet a client you *didn't* like. You do know we can't save them all, right?"

"Way to have a positive outlook there, Adeline." Olivia threw her hands up in the air. "Debbie downer...she delivers."

"Say what you want, Olivia, but it's shit like Greg Delaney that use their connections to rule with an iron fist. He will make an example out of us and his wife."

"Okay, Adeline, we've heard your side." Melanie turned her attention to Sunday. "What are your thoughts?"

Sunday shrugged. "I've got a feeling, I'll have the votes on my side."

Adeline scoffed. "Livi, what do you think?"

"Politician's wife. Payment shouldn't be a problem."

Melanie chewed on her lower lip. "Maybe. . .then again he could be keeping her on a tight leash."

"Love is the issue with her, not money." Sunday defended her stance.

Adeline shook her head. "We don't know that. Hell, for all we know Loren could be a great liar and actress."

"Adeline, let Loren worry about how Loren pays, okay? We've got shit to do, as long as she can cover the deposit. Besides, there's always Coco's."

"Thank god for Coco," they all said in unison. Coco was the owner of Queen's Gold a notorious pawn shop in downtown Orlando.

"Coco may not be all that willing to help Loren though, you know how she feels about cops. I don't think she holds much more respect for our Mayor Greg Delaney either."

"Well, depending on the vote, let's see what Loren comes up with first," Sunday explained.

"Sounds to me that Sunday is in favor of helping Loren. Is that right?" Melanie turned to Sunday and Sunday nodded.

"Who else is in favor of Loren?" Melanie held up her hand along with Olivia.

"Not me." Adeline was the only one not agreeing. Everyone turned to stare at Adeline amazed since she usually was the first one to want to defend all women.

"You've got a knack for being the odd one, don't you?" Melanie shook her head, once again shocked by Adeline.

"What? I don't like politicians. They're grabby. They're self-righteous, and chances are I'll have to get up close and personal with this one." Adeline shivered at the thought.

"Well, I say that we help her. She needs us and it is our

job to help those that need us. Will it be risky? Yes, but that will only help us in the long run. We will prove hands down that no one in Central Florida is above us or above being busted by us. Think about it, the rumor mill that will be sparked at who actually caught Greg Delaney red-handed?"

"How about you, Olivia?"

"She's got a kid. If it was just her, then I'd weigh whether or not it was worth going against someone who had that much power and money but there's a kid involved. We do it."

Adeline flicked her nails nonchalantly as though it was no big deal that the others weren't agreeing with her. "What about you, Mel? What are your thoughts?"

"I think that while we are getting evidence to help protect Loren that we gather a little extra to protect ourselves. You know? Call it an insurance policy. He comes after us, then no matter what happens between him and Loren we have material to ruin him."

Sunday clapped her hands together. "Let's catch the lyin' lion."

"Outfox the fox," Olivia added.

"A lion wouldn't cheat but a Tiger Wood."

"Ohhh, that was badddd." They all groaned and turned to Adeline.

"What?" Adeline asked, feigning surprise. "Why are you looking at me?"

The other three let out sighs. Whether they admitted it or not, they all kind of loved Adeline just the way she was.

"Since the majority has spoken you know the rules and will have to learn to cope with your feelings. It is all hands on deck. We're going to have to do more digging than usual. I have a feeling that Mayor Delaney is especially skilled at hiding his tracks." Everyone agreed with Melanie's announcement.

"Sunday?" Melanie went down her list of notes she'd made.

"Yes, Homie?"

"You're gonna arrange a meeting with Loren at the country club, you're also gonna let her know about our retainer fee."

"At least make it our elevated fee," Adeline chimed in.

"Fifteen thousand?" Sunday asked.

Adeline nodded and so did Melanie and Olivia.

"Consider it done." Sunday gave a mock salute.

"Tires and bullets aren't cheap these days, you know? And besides we're not messing around on this one," Adeline defended her reasoning.

"Everyone got their jobs?" Melanie looked at Olivia and Adeline.

"I'll head over toward the mayor's office and start scouting the area. I'll upload photos as soon as I discover anything of use."

"I'll start trying to find out where he hangs out and if he's in to brunettes?" Adeline patted her perfectly coifed hair as she headed out to her car.

More than anything Adeline would like to throw on a helmet and straddle a motorcycle but that was unladylike and part of their formula for success was to maintain an elevated lady-like appearance in public. Her only public rebellion was her cars. Adeline blamed it on *tools of the trade*. As the lead tactical driver and instructor for evasive driving maneuvers, Adeline claimed to need powerful cars and nothing screamed power like good old American heavy duty V8 muscle cars. Plus, often times they provided the added bonus of opening conversations with their targets.

Adeline pulled into a parking lot across from City Hall and parked. Sliding on her Zoomies, one of the greatest inventions for a private eye or peeping tom, take your pick, since the hands free binoculars looked like nothing more than ordinary glasses. Adeline reclined a bit in her seat, turned on her tunes, and watched the front doors and parking lot of the mayor's office. She needed to establish a routine for the mayor.

48792136R00124

Made in the USA
Columbia, SC
12 January 2019